Kira and the Ice Storm

Francisco Angulo de Lafuente

Published by Francisco Angulo de Lafuente, 2023.

KIRA AND THE ICE STORM

First edition. August 22, 2023.

ISBN: 979-8223769767

Written by Francisco Angulo de Lafuente.

Table of Contents

KIRA AND THE ICE STORM

****WARNING****

This is a science fiction novel.

THE DATA AND SCIENTIFIC theories extracted from the diaries and notebooks of Agnux may not be valid in our space-time.

Agnux's manuscripts are much more complicated than this book. I have dedicated many years to their study and deciphering; but new hidden data always appears. They are complex documents, mostly encrypted. Some of his letters seem normal at first glance, but under their appearance there are countless coded messages that reveal information about his discoveries.

After reading the warnings, I must warn you that this book delves into the complexity of relativistic theories; creating paradoxes that can lead to reader confusion. Time does not have to follow a line, it can make sudden changes creating several parallel realities. In other words: the right path can be any. In fact even more than one at a time. Up and down, right and left at the same time. Everything depends on the observer's point of view. In this story you, the reader, are the viewer and your conclusions, even if they differ from mine and even Agnux's, will be the right ones.

You will meet protagonists who live in the past, others are in the future and even some who coexist in several timelines. I ask for your effort and attention so that you can satisfactorily resolve this story, placing each character in their rightful place. If you find yourself reading on the train or in an unfavorable place, you may have to reread part or all of this book to fit the pieces that open the doors of this sphere.

Foreword

KIRA AND THE ICE STORM transports us back into Angulo's chilling literary landscape, where an otherworldly ice storm of apocalyptic proportions threatens to freeze all life as we know it.

Critics and fans alike have been eagerly awaiting Angulo's latest offering. His previous works garnered much acclaim, with the Los Angeles Times declaring that Angulo "breathes life into fictional worlds more captivating than our own." Meanwhile, the Chicago Tribune dubbed him "the next giant of speculative fiction."

Indeed, Angulo's books have built him a devoted cult following. The electrifying plot twists and propulsive action of his novels leave readers grasping their book covers white-knuckled. Yet beyond the exhilarating sci-fi trappings, Angulo imbues his work with philosophical depth and moral resonance.

At the heart of the series is Kira, the fiercely intelligent and courageous heroine who anchors these stories. With Kira and the Ice Storm, Angulo has woven another thought-provoking tale exploring fundamental questions of humanity and existence, all while keeping readers racing through pages well past their bedtimes.

Angulo's scrupulous attention to scientific plausibility and research into futuristic technologies bring a stark realism to his works, heightening the sense of impending dread. While disaster awaits, hope endures in the unbreakable human spirit embodied by Kira as she and her band of fellow survivors navigate unimaginable threats.

So brace yourselves as Angulo ushers us again to the brink of ruin and back. But no matter how icy the tempest, Kira's flame never wavers. And Angulo fans wouldn't have it any other way.

KIRA WOKE UP BEFORE the alarm went off, which was very unusual since she tended to sleep like a log. Her deep sleep was hard to interrupt and very often the alarm would ring for several minutes. Today the thunder and lightning from a strong electric storm had woken her up earlier than usual. It was the most spectacular storm she had ever seen; lightning was striking everywhere. One bolt hit her apartment building, making the foundations tremble. She wasn't afraid of them, but it was one thing to watch a storm and quite another to be under this huge black cloud incessantly unleashing lightning bolts.

After that, as always, the rush – no time to get properly ready and have a decent breakfast. She'd drink a glass of cold coffee and rush out at full speed. Even though it was hard for her to wake up and she always had to bolt out of the house towards the Hospital, she had never been late for work. The same could not be said for most of the doctors.

Since she was little she had wanted to be a doctor and it had been very difficult for her to get where she was now. For others, for her colleagues it hadn't been so hard, but she came from a humble family. There were certainly poorer ones. Although money has nothing to do with intelligence, it makes things much easier when it comes to being able to study at a good school. People tend to be very wrong about this, since they often think that people make themselves on their own. Nothing could be further from the truth. You can't just abandon a child on the street, among the dregs of society, and expect them to come back at twenty-five as an engineer. For someone to learn to play the piano, they first need to have a piano. Kira knew very well from experience how hard it is to learn an instrument when you don't have one. She had to make her own way. Not only did no one guide her, quite the contrary, they tried to convince her that she was wrong. What was the point of having impossible dreams like becoming a doctor? The sooner she came back down to earth the better, her family thought. She had many confrontations with her parents. As soon as she got home, you could feel the tension in the air. Instead of feeling proud, they felt offended, resentful, as if she had switched sides. Her father despised any man who didn't earn a living with a pick and shovel. For him, all those people were despicable beings, pen pushers as he called them. They felt a kind of hatred towards their daughter for having betrayed them; not only that, she also made them feel inferior. Not all parents want their children to become king, some don't want to give up their throne. In any case, they never believed she would finish her studies, let alone become a surgeon. Of course, if her father didn't even know how to tie his shoes, his daughter couldn't be much smarter. She might fool outsiders, but she wouldn't fool him.

Be that as it may, Kira was an exception. One of those genetic miracles that happens every now and then. To really be a doctor you need to have a vocation, since it's a complicated career and you have to spend several years doing internships before you can practice. Most students drop out in the first year. It becomes very hard having to become familiar with illnesses and death. In the first course, cadaver dissection practices are continuously carried out. But this was never a problem for her.

Spring was coming to an end, the days were longer and the weather during the past week had been summery. The storm was quite shocking. She thought that days like these were good for staying home. She opened the closet and threw some clothes on the bed, then got dressed as if she were running late. She grabbed a gentleman's black umbrella, she didn't have another one since she normally didn't use any. As she left the house, hail started falling heavily. Balls of ice the size of golf balls. Parked cars that were hit by the frozen raindrops seemed to complain, setting off their alarms. Kira took refuge in the first shop she came across. Inside, multitudes of pedestrians were doing the same. They were all talking nonstop, commenting on what was happening. It's curious how in these moments people become closer. In big cities most people don't even greet each other, even if they are neighbors; but in an extraordinary event everyone starts chatting as if they were old acquaintances. It seems that often difficulties reveal a bit of the humanity of those urbanites who live like ants. Perhaps, if we could solve everything by our own means and never needed help from others, we would cease to be human, becoming a kind of unfeeling robotic being.

The damage to street furniture and cars continued to increase, which seemed to make some people happy. I'm not quite sure if they were laughing at other people's misfortune or enjoying watching their car get pummeled by the hail. In some cases, one can feel relief watching their vehicle, that they have to pay a bitter monthly fee for, being destroyed by the hail.

Just as it started, it ended in the blink of an eye. Now the sound of the hailstones was replaced only by the honking car alarms; in a few seconds these stopped and only the murmur of the crowd crammed into the store could be heard. Everyone talked about what had happened. Then they fell silent like a wind-up toy running out of batteries. A few minutes later there was absolute silence; everyone changed their faces, as if they had put on masks, and left the premises. Once again they returned to their normal state, like bees after the rain.

The accumulated hail on the ground formed a solid layer several centimeters thick that turned the streets into skating rinks. A car turned the corner, driving too fast for the conditions. Its windows were cracked from the storm and you couldn't quite see who was driving it. It approached at high speed towards the door of the shop where there were still many people. It tried to turn right, but the tires lost traction and it continued moving while spinning. At the moment Kira said watch out, the SUV plowed into the pedestrians. Screams were heard and she ran over to see what happened. Between several people they picked up an individual who was under the vehicle. Others berated the driver, pounding on the bodywork. Fearing he would get lynched, the driver engaged the locks. He was a middle-aged, obese, very pale-skinned man dotted with freckles.

On the ground lay an unconscious young man due to the injuries sustained in the collision.

"He killed him!" shouted one of the older women in the crowd. Without hesitation the doctor approached and checked the young man's pulse by placing her index and middle fingers on his neck. When she pressed the carotid artery she felt his weak pulse. He was breathing with difficulty. She examined him quickly and was able to confirm her worst fears. The victim had suffered a concussion from the impact; but worst of all, his broken ribs, as a bone fragment was embedded in his lung. It was a very delicate, extremely urgent situation, because if he wasn't stabilized immediately, his lungs would flood with blood and fluid, drowning him. She grabbed her phone to call an ambulance, but only heard a message indicating lack of coverage. Several people who formed a circle around her offered their phones.

"Try this one, this company always has coverage," said a man as he held out his hand to offer it to her. She dialed emergency services again, but the same recording played.

"Call emergency, we need to get him to a hospital immediately."

Everyone took out their phones and called the different emergency services. The result was the same.

It seemed unbelievable that they were all out of service. Perhaps the storm had affected a large area and the hard hailstones could have destroyed the telephone relay antennas.

"I, I, I here, I here," stammered the Asian featured shop owner, barely able to speak. He meant that he had a landline phone in the store. A man ran inside and grabbed the handset in one hand, getting ready to press the keypad with the other. Before pressing any buttons, he heard a voice. Apparently the shopkeeper had already called the hospital, but they couldn't understand him. The problem now was that emergency services were saturated; the emergency room kept receiving injured people and the few ambulances still in service were trapped on streets and roads due to the large number of accidents. The entire city infrastructure seemed to have collapsed due to the storm.

"There's no time to lose; if we don't stabilize him in the next few minutes we'll lose him. The normal thing would be to give him a bottle of serum and a blood plasma bag to try to raise his pulse by replenishing the blood lost. But we don't have any of those things here. I'm going to have to take a chance using experimental techniques. Instead of trying to get him back to a normal rhythm, I'll try to get his heart to continue beating below normal.

It was no time for doubts, and although what she was about to do would be disapproved of by most of her colleagues, there was no other choice in this situation; of course, it's best to try to implement a technique that has only been tested on mice than to stand there with arms crossed.

"Bring a couple bags of ice and a bottle of mineral water," she asked the shop owner, who without hesitation ran for them. Although he barely understood our language, he was completely familiar with all the names of the products he had in his store.

"Does anyone have neuralgia?"

They all looked at each other in surprise: What did it matter now if someone had a headache?

"I, I suffer from migraines," said the lady who was monitoring the pulse without stopping marking it.

"What else do you suffer from?"

She began to list, without stopping indicating the pulse, a series of endless ailments. Kira knew that middle-aged women and up seemed to collect diseases; trying to impress the neighbors, as if it were a poker game, where each one ups the ante with a more serious condition. Most of the illnesses were caused by age and boredom. She remembered very well her years of practice, having to hold clinic for patients who were only looking for conversation, and who weren't satisfied until they were diagnosed with a new condition. Luckily, her intuition didn't fail and that woman was a walking pharmacy; she had her purse overflowing with medication. She dumped the contents onto the counter, right next to the victim's head.

"Let's see: Pain relievers, anti-inflammatories... Lidocaine, Acetaminophen, Acetylsalicylic Acid, liquid Epinephrine..."

With some of the products she prepared a mixture inside the mineral water bottle; then she screwed the cap back on and pierced it with a key. She covered his chest with ice to lower his body temperature; this would put the patient into shock, his heart would beat slower and she could prevent him from bleeding out. At the same time he would remain unconscious, which was essential to perform the operation.

"I need: scissors, tweezers, a sharp knife. I also need someone to cut off the plug of the fan and remove the wire without breaking the casing."

She used the hollow plastic tube that coated the metal wire as a probe. She forcibly inserted one end into the hole in the container holding the medication mixture. She greased the other end in butter and inserted it into his nose until it reached his stomach. She ordered one of the assistants to hold him upside down. The liquid flowed drop by drop through the duct, supplying him with a steady dose. It would have been much more effective to administer it intravenously, but she didn't have a catheter. She bent the metal rod into an oval shape for the head; then she used a piece of rubber tubing as a splint. She palpated his side, examining the young man, and marked several crosses with a marker. She picked up the improvised scalpel, and at that moment Tim, paler than a snowflake, swallowed hard trying to keep his composure. The doctor sank the knife blade into his side at one of the marked points. Tim staggered, rolling his eyes in line with his face. But before collapsing, Kira dealt him a resounding slap on both cheeks, making him instantly regain his color and consciousness. Even so he continued trembling and swaying, with the characteristic floppiness of a puppet's limbs.

TODAY I HAD DIFFICULTY getting out of bed, my head was spinning so I took an aspirin. Then, in the bathroom, I washed my face with plenty of cold water. Looking at myself in the mirror I was amazed at my image. I looked great, much younger.

I could remember last night's dream in great detail. It was clear it hadn't been a normal dream.

After clearing my head a bit I returned to the bedroom. She was resting peacefully in bed. She had such a pretty little face! How I had missed her! I watched her sleep for a while, then lay down next to her again, hugging her. I loved having her in my arms. My chest against her back and my head close to hers, able to smell the sweet aroma of her hair. I spent the rest of the morning like that until she woke up.

During breakfast I leafed through the Sunday paper as usual. The date: May 4th. That meant there were 471 days left. I remembered that number and smiled. Life is definitely much more complicated than we can imagine. But as a good friend told me once: Nothing is left to chance, God doesn't play dice.

THE MACHINE ADVANCED along the asphalt street, leaving the imprint of its track links. Its engine roared and its black exhaust breath left a dark cloud behind. Its articulated arm shaped like a claw at the end gave it a hellish look, a gigantic steel monster that moved slowly toward the old building.

Its driver, a fifty-year-old man with a brutish appearance, gray hair only in some areas and reddish skin, held a plastic pipe between his teeth that he kept moving from side to side in his mouth.

"God! What a day! What day did I choose to quit smoking!" he murmured, trying to suck on that ridiculous fake cigarette.

The wrecker kept getting closer and closer to the people holding protest signs against the demolition. Certainly this kind of incident didn't happen every day, but today it seemed impossible for the demolition to take place, which frayed the Bear's nerves even more. He normally smoked between two and three packs of cigarettes a day, and that very morning he had bought some of those ridiculous toy cigarettes to quit smoking. His body didn't seem to be responding well to the lack of nicotine, and at times he was unable to react properly. The machine kept advancing toward the crowd and when they were just a few meters apart, the driver abruptly accelerated. The Bear's eyes fixed on the crowd and chewing that fake cigarette he lost control of the mammoth wrecker. The group of protesters turned pale when they saw themselves already under the huge tracks on which that monster moved. The man reacted just in time to stop the contraption a few scarce centimeters from the crowd. Immediately, the people gathered there began to hurl all kinds of verbal abuse followed by objects that impacted the cabin windows behind which he was taking shelter. Thanks to the quick intervention of the police he was able to get out of that mob, albeit not without taking some blows and even several hair pulls dealt by the furious women who were part of the protesters.

Although they called him Bear, he was no burly man, rather small and chubby. Since he lacked a waist due to his protruding belly, he always had to wear a belt to keep his pants up. The belt was always buckled to the very last hole, since he wore it underneath his belly, because on top of his round gut it was totally impossible to keep it fastened; of course by wearing his pants so low, as soon as he bent over, his ass was exposed. So you can imagine the spectacle: the protesters pulling him one way and the law enforcement officers pulling the other, the Bear with his privates exposed, that ass so white it shone in the sunlight like a reflective safety vest.

"I'm going home; if the officers don't disperse this group of retards, I'll leave Manuela where she is and let's see who's brave enough to lay a finger on her!" the man said very annoyed looking at the group of guards.

They argued heatedly for a long time; the neighbors were unwilling to demolish the building, which for them was historic and almost world heritage. How stupid! he thought, since he had demolished much older buildings. Finally, the big shots, the company executives, agreed to assess the condition of the property. They called him on the phone and, accompanied by two policemen, they entered the lobby. The building was near Independence Square and seemed to date back to the same time. It was all a mere ploy on the part of the multinational corporation, because the laborer was no expert and his opinion was worthless; in fact, the decision had already been made: the demolition would continue its course. At the back of the lobby, just to the right of the utility room door, there was another, metal one, with a heavy padlock guarding it. They asked the neighbors, but none of them knew where it led. This made the man hesitate: if he had to demolish the building he had to know for certain what was behind that door. If a catastrophe occurred he would be held responsible. It could be an illegal workshop where immigrants worked. Although the door seemed to have been unopened for a long time. But it could also connect to the underground metro tunnels, and if they didn't take this into account when demolishing the homes, they could cause property damage of incalculable value, and the Bear didn't have any insurance to cover these types of issues.

"It'd be best to open the door; if no one has the key I'll open it with my hydraulic shears."

No sooner said than done; they opened the entrance with difficulty and saw the long descending corridor. This was more serious than it seemed, he thought, and although not without hesitation, they had to go down and take a look. Only one of the officers had a flashlight. They walked a good distance to a place where the underground branched off. Given the complexity of that place, the best thing was to leave and put the case in expert hands. To their surprise, on the way back, they realized that the tunnel showed multitudes of branches that they had left behind without realizing it as they walked.

"I'm sure it's the entrance on the right and my sense of direction never fails."

"I think it's the center one," one of the policemen disagreed.

They couldn't agree and when it came to stubbornness no one could beat the Bear. He took the path to the right and the police took the center one. But none of them guessed right and all three ventured into that underground labyrinth.

"Damn my luck, I can't see three feet in front of me," he cursed as he clumsily walked, feeling the damp walls with his hand. In the distance he saw a faint light.

"I knew it; my instinct never fails; I won't be able to stop laughing when they have to send a rescue team to get those two idiots out."

He quickened his pace, thinking the light he saw came from the outside; but when he realized it, he was in a huge room, where a strange machine connected to multitudes of cables produced the luminous effect inside.

"Is anyone there? Come out guys I heard you. Now is not the time for games..."

15

NORMALLY, IT DOESN'T take me long to come up with a story, and in just a few hours, I can imagine what the plot of the novel will be; after that, the hard work begins, doing research and slowly getting into the storyline. Creation is complex, because for days, weeks, months and even years, I'm constantly thinking about the work, not as a fictional fable; I think of it as if it were a true story, as if it were part of my memories. I walk down the street lost, disoriented, immersed in the mind of each of the characters, thinking about how each one of them would act.

The other day I was walking quite fast with my hands in my pockets, since it was very cold, the wind was blowing hard and I had to continually wrestle with it, as I moved back and forth across the sidewalk. I walked with my head down, thinking about how time would pass differently in different systems; I imagined myself on the surface of a large planet, where gravity was several times greater than ours, a world in a distant galaxy. The sound of a car horn slightly diverted my attention, making me turn my head to look at the vehicle that was on the roadway, but I quickly continued immersed in my thoughts; I immediately turned my face forward again and felt a sharp, cold, metallic sound that echoed in the air as I separated my face from the iron frame of that lamppost. A moment later, I looked up and down the whole street and I can certify that more than one person had seen me smash into it. I thought only my pride was hurt; but a few seconds later a strong headache, almost made me lose my balance and with difficulty I continued walking in a casual manner so as not to draw the attention of passersby. A few steps later I began to suspect that something was wrong; people stared at my face, as if I had an insult written on my forehead. Instinctively I paid more attention to where they were looking and I noticed something wet sliding down my face. I touched my cheek with my fingers and after feeling them wet I looked at them closely and I could see how the tips were stained red. Blood was gushing from my eyebrow and dripping from my chin in spurts, leaving a trail of drops along the sidewalk. I had to get something to stop the bleeding and clean the wound, but I only had my backpack with me with the library books I was going to return. I took out one of the texts and even thinking about what explanations I could give the librarian, I started by tearing out a page and wiped my face with it; then I kept putting several of them against my eyebrow and pressing with my hands. Now that the conditions seemed to be under control, I analyzed the situation and felt quite ridiculous with my face plastered with relativistic theories. The first thing was to get home, properly treat the cut on my forehead and then I'd think about how to deal with the matter of the books.

I walked back home trying not to draw attention to myself and looking in the distance, with the eye that wasn't covered by the pages, I made out a familiar figure.

"What happened to you? Why do you have half your face wrapped in papers?"

I couldn't believe it; I just happened to run into one of the girls who worked at the library. I began stammering before being able to articulate a word; I was thinking about how to give a quick plausible explanation, and if possible, the least humiliating one possible. As I tend to think very slowly, I could do nothing but tell the truth, that I was distracted thinking about my stuff, and when I realized it I found myself face first against the pole.

"Let me look at the wound."

"No, no, don't worry, it's nothing."

She insisted on uncovering the gash. She told me it would be best if I went to the doctor to get a few stitches, as the cut seemed quite deep.

What an awkward situation. Now, more than the bump what bothered me was having to waste the day at the clinic. I've always had a real aversion to health centers.

"Come on, don't think about it anymore, I have nothing to do right now and I can go with you."

Now things were beginning to take on a different color. Thanks to the blow, I managed to get her attention, and although it was just about accompanying me to the emergency room, for me it was almost like a date.

Work was the center of my life and I never paid attention to other things. Up to now I never noticed any girl.

We took a bus that stopped at the doctor's office and entered the emergency room waiting area. As usual, it was packed. People suffering from different ailments awaited their turn sitting in long rows of seats; arranged as if in a movie theater. Looking at their faces you could guess their ailments, which caused me tremendous anguish. Feverish faces, jaundiced faces, gastroenteritis faces, blue, yellow, purple faces, pale faces... Certainly this was not the best place to be. But for the first time in my life I didn't care about that scenario. I was totally absorbed in the conversation with my lovely companion.

It was our turn and we both went into the office. She and the practitioner knew each other and they started chatting, so I just stood there looking like an idiot, staring back and forth at them, waiting for them to stop ignoring me. Apparently the doctor gave lectures at the university and that's where they met. It's curious how in the blink of an eye, you go from feeling like the center of the universe and the luckiest person in the world to feeling completely excluded. Of course, since you don't know people well, you try to listen to the conversation to see if there's a gap you can chime into; but since you also don't want to seem obtrusive, the situation gets complicated. If you don't talk, bad deal, because they'll say this guy is very quiet. I think he's a little weird; and if you interrupt you become an annoying jerk. I watched her carefully and she seemed to drift farther away.

"And what happened to you? Didn't math make sense? Was it a fighting book...?"

I had to put up with his stupid jokes throughout the entire exam. Finally, they didn't stitch me up; he put a kind of sticker on. Thank goodness, because I probably would have fainted if he pricked me with a needle and given him even more fodder for his ridiculous jokes. When we left, and I was already counting on everything being lost, I said goodbye and thought about getting back to work as soon as possible. But she invited me for coffee.

"Sorry for the bad time. The doctor is my teacher and even though he's stupid I have to put up with him."

We talked and talked the whole time, about all kinds of things; we discussed our proposals for improving the world, our concerns, projects, etc...

I don't remember half of what I said and I don't even drink alcohol; I was surprising myself saying some silly things, which later, mentally re-examining the conversation, I felt embarrassed about. Finally, when the time came to say goodbye, I didn't know how to say it, I thought that if I gave her a hug, it might seem too clingy, so I shook her hand, as if she were one of my colleagues. She looked at me a little surprised; maybe she thought I didn't want anything with her, or, even worse, that she took me for a homosexual. Then I would become the confessor friend and would have to put up with her stories about ex-boyfriends for the rest of my life. Since I wasn't saying anything she said:

"See you tomorrow at seven at the library door. Muah!"

She kissed me on the mouth and left. I was so excited I almost started dancing; in fact, I went home quietly singing without realizing it, until I noticed some people staring at me.

What nerves, what stress! I didn't know what to do to make the hours go by. I tried to read, but I couldn't concentrate; I pretended to sleep but nothing, my eyes wouldn't close, I spent all my time remembering that kiss over and over again. Already at dawn, and unable to sleep at all, with the pillow deformed from hugging it so much, I had to get up and make myself some linden tea to calm down.

The next day, two hours before the meeting, I was already ready, freshly showered and dressed; I didn't know what to do; so I sat watching the seconds hand slowly advance. After an hour that seemed like a year to me, I thought it would be better to leave the house and walk slowly to the library, but no matter how slowly I tried to walk, time didn't pass; so forty minutes before the date, there I was, at the door, like an idiot watching everyone go by. Maybe I should have bought her flowers, or a small gift; women usually like those kinds of things. But even though they like thoughtful men, they often contradict themselves by calling them annoying. Maybe it's not necessary for today, maybe tomorrow I could give her a rose? No, no, a rose would seem too commitment oriented: girls today don't want to get into that kind of mess; better something less serious, a CD of her favorite band. I was standing there at the door continuously rambling and arguing with myself, for a moment I thought they were going to call me crazy and call the police, but the older female security guard with a butcher's build, shook her head from side to side while disdainfully looking at me. She'd think: what a fool...

Finally, the clock struck seven; not much time left; I looked back and forth, making sure no one saw me and straightened my shirt and pants smoothing them with my palm. Minutes passed and nothing, no one appeared; finally, I saw her come down the steps leading to the building lobby. I tried to keep my composure, but I felt like jumping.

"Calm down, calm down, don't smile, don't raise your eyebrows, relax your facial muscles," I said quietly to myself trying not to look like an idiot. But as soon as she crossed the threshold, I lost control and made the typical stupid face of someone in love.

THE PATIENT HAD LOST a lot of blood. The operation seemed to be going well, all the assistants had to help in one way or another. His pulse began to drop and his heart stopped beating.

"Don't die... come on, fight a little, come on, 1001, 1002, 1003, breathe," Kira yelled while performing resuscitation maneuvers. She pressed hard on his chest with her hands and gave him mouth-to-mouth.

The boy suddenly opened his eyes and abruptly took in air, as if he'd been holding his breath for minutes. Then he continued breathing slowly and his eyelids closed again. Then the doctor held his face in her hands, to lift him up.

"Look at me, don't close your eyes, make an effort. Come on!, come on!, let's go! You have to stay conscious. What's your name?"

The young man tried to speak, but nothing could be heard. She came closer so he could whisper in her ear. He whispered something, which the others didn't hear.

The patient seemed stabilized, but he needed to be taken to a hospital as soon as possible. Those gathered there didn't dare open the doors of the store. Outside, it seemed to be night, the wind was blowing so hard that it dragged all kinds of objects. Various debris fell from the facades of buildings. A huge blow exploded the tank of one of the cars parked at the edge of the sidewalk. An enormous air conditioner had fallen from above, impacting the vehicle. Flames erupted like volleys of fire for a few moments, but the freezing wind managed to extinguish the fire. Literally, the fuel, gasoline and air that fed that fire became frozen. Inside a van parked across the street, you could see a woman and her eight year old daughter taking shelter inside. The objects dragged by the strong wind struck the windows. The place wasn't safe; if they wanted to survive, they would have to get out of the vehicle and find a safer shelter. A planter violently broke through the rear window. The woman wanted to get out grabbing her daughter's arm. But they shouted from the store for her to stay put. It was impossible, no one could walk in that storm; nor was it possible to move forward much before being struck by some object turned into a projectile. The situation couldn't be worse: if they stayed in the car they would freeze to death in a short time, that is if something didn't fall on them and crush them.

"We have to go, get them out, we have to bring them here," said the store owner. And he prepared to go out. Then they stopped him, preventing him from opening the doors of the business. Some were afraid the man wouldn't come back, others were afraid something would happen to them by leaving the door open.

"Let me, I'll go out," said a voice from the back of the store. Everyone turned to see who it was. It was a strong young man, clad with a sheet metal bucket on his head, with reinforcements all over his body like armor. He had kitchen utensils adhered to his body with packing tape, pans and other stuff. He tied one end of a rope around his waist and gave the other end to the people at the door.

"I'm going out; hold the rope tight so the wind doesn't carry me away."

He was barely finishing saying these words when he found himself across the street from the entrance. The people inside held the door ajar, leaving enough space to pass the rope through. The man outside leaned forward struggling against the wind, trying to stay on his feet. Even with all the weight he carried, the strong gusts dragged him from side to side, shaking him like a leaf. The effort was tremendous; loaded down with the heavy costume and that iron bucket on his head, he looked like a medieval knight in armor. He made some holes in the bucket, through which he could see. Inside he could only hear the sound of his breathing.

"Watch out!" the people in the store shouted, but with the noise of the wind and the metal helmet, he couldn't hear anything. A roof tile came straight at his head from the cornice. Everyone closed their eyes for a few seconds so as not to see the huge blow. But when they opened them the man was still standing, with the dented armor, but as if nothing had happened. He continued with great difficulty, until reaching the other side of the street. He opened the door of the van with effort; he went inside and came back out holding the two women. He tried to walk against the gale to get back to the shop as soon as possible, walking backwards, to shield the mother and daughter with his body. But no matter how hard he tried, they couldn't make any progress. From the store they tried to reel in the line, but the weight was too much, the rope slipped burning their hands. The young man in armor realized this and they returned to the vehicle. He tied them up tightly and armed them with some of his protections. They went back outside and this time the plan did seem to work. They pulled the rope hard and managed to bring the women to the shelter of the premises. The savior was now in a precarious situation. Without a rope he would likely be swept away by the tornado; but if he stayed in the car, he would soon die of cold, if he didn't do so earlier due to debris. He got out of the car and took a step toward the store.

"Come on, come on, one more step..." they encouraged him from the shop; but when he took the third step he lost his balance and rolled on the ground until disappearing down the street.

Silence fell among the survivors. It was suddenly broken by Kira's calm, steady voice.

"Hurry, the glass is cracking, it won't hold much longer, we have to reinforce the entrance."

They took bags of dog food, bags of salt, rice and legumes and barricaded the entrance, reinforcing it with a wall of products on sale.

Outside, the storm darkened the sky so much that only the lights on through the windows of some houses could be seen. The light bulbs began to sputter and then went out. Someone used a lighter as a flashlight and searched the shelves.

"Bingo!" He grabbed some candles and lit them.

A tall, thin older man rummaged nervously among the shelves. Finally, he found something and put it in the pocket of his shirt. Then he approached the doctor and spoke to her unintelligibly, he was very nervous.

"Miss, I need to take my medicine or I'll die, my ulcer will start bleeding and I know I'll die; yes I will finally die, if I don't take my medicine. We're all going to die! This is God's punishment. Only the pure of heart will be saved, like in the Biblical flood. It's, it's a shame I'm an atheist, because atheists surely won't be saved. What god is going to save me? If at least I were Buddhist..."

"Take a bag, put it on your face and breathe. What's your name?"

"Sa...muel!" the man articulated while sitting on the floor without removing the bag from his face.

The injured man was lying on top of the counter, with his head slightly raised, using a package of bags as a pillow. The dim light of the candles lit up the room where some twenty people took refuge; most were grouped in small circles, sitting on the floor, leaning against the perimeter walls, whispering, talking quietly among themselves. Another group, the most active, was at the door, near the counter, doing anything Kira ordered them: Handing out blankets and warm clothing, looking on the shelves for the most useful items, flashlights, raincoats and anything else to keep their spirits up, like some candy and chocolate.

"Hey, look what I found!" said David, as he headed toward the group at a brisk pace holding something in his hands. It was an old radio, one of the old-fashioned kind. It may seem like a fairly common object, but the truth is that you see fewer and fewer of them, since most people listen to the radio in their cars or on computers. Digital broadcasts are beating out old analog stations. He put it on the counter, a couple of meters from the patient, and pressed all the buttons trying to find the power button. A circle of people formed around him and one reached in, nervously grabbed the device and removed the back cover. He put batteries in the compartment and it started playing. Without even tuning it or touching the dial, a voice was automatically heard saying:

"The authorities have declared a state of emergency, no one leave their homes. Try to take shelter with provisions in a safe place. I repeat, no one leave their homes. Remain in your homes."

Apparently, the situation was more complicated than it seemed. Far from any forecast, the authorities and state security forces were being overwhelmed by events. Simply put, they were not prepared to deal with a situation like the one before them. The freezing wind froze absolutely everything, turning trees, turrets, telephone poles, antennas, etc., into phantasmagoric ice sculptures, fragile as crystal. The huge power pylons yielded under the weight of the icebergs hanging like icicles. Like the giant Goliath, they were felled, shattering into a thousand pieces upon hitting the ground.

The small mercury thermometer, hanging on the wall under the clock, couldn't even reach the first tick mark. The breathing of the people expelled a cloud of steam that froze almost instantly, settling on any surface. Everything shone, as if covered by a layer of fine crystal. They seemed to be in one of those huge walk-in freezers that large supermarkets have. The groups of people drew closer together due to the cold. Finally a single ensemble, covered with blankets, towels, kitchen rags and anything else that could be used as coats, tried to withstand it together. Seeing that the situation was worsening by the minute, Kira decided that the best thing was to go out and try to reach a better equipped place. She had to try by all possible means to get the injured to a hospital, but also thinking of the others.

"We have to get out of the store and walk down the street; the Santa Maria school is down there, where people took shelter during the floods of '31. There we'll be safe; we can meet up with our relatives, have a hot soup and get medical care for those who need it."

"I, I, I thi,thi,think it's, it's be,be,better if we, we, we st,stay," Tim stuttered, half frozen. He continued saying they'd be safer in the store than anywhere else. Many began having doubts. The cold prevented them from thinking clearly and most were starting to give up. A foolish idea lingered in their minds: they thought if they took a nap, they'd wake up invigorated. Some even thought it must all be a bad dream and any moment they'd wake up lying in their beds. But nothing could be further from reality.

The doctor had to take control again to get the crowd's attention. She wouldn't let that foolish comfort convince the others and end up with them all dying.

They placed the patient on an improvised stretcher and positioned him in the center of the group. They tied themselves at the waist with a rope, shielding themselves with buckets, trash cans, pots, lids. The idea was to advance like an army of Roman legionnaires, forming a compact group, with the strongest on the outside and sheltering the weakest on the inside. They dismantled the barricade covering the door and unlatched the bolt joining the two doors. The wind pushed the doors wide open. Tim, who up to now had been sitting on the floor, with a blanket over his head, and eating candy nonstop, jumped to his feet when he saw they were serious about leaving him alone in the store. He moved his huge butt so fast that before anyone could say anything to him he was inside the rope tying them together. They then advanced slowly, struggling against the blizzard. The debris, launched by the elements with bad intentions, collided against the protections they were holding up with their arms. Their limbs complained from the barrage of blows. No matter how hard Aeolus tried to knock them down with his gusts, the armadillo-looking platoon managed to stay on their feet, slowly progressing toward 43rd street. With great difficulty they reached the intersection. The avenue that descended to the school was full of junk everywhere. The large business signs had collapsed and wrecked cars could be seen in the most absurd places. There were vehicles inside some storefronts, some on top of others, even one perched on a balcony, five meters off the ground. Visibility wasn't great, you could only see about 100 or 200 meters, but enough to get an idea of how difficult it would be for them to cross that battlefield.

"Tac, tactac, tac, trac, trac..."

They heard this metallic sound striking the asphalt. A strange noise that started with a single emitter which was quickly joined by more, until hundreds or thousands could be heard. It wasn't clear what it was, but whatever it was, it was coming down 43rd fast and would soon catch up to them. The uproar that formed paralyzed the entire group. They opened a gap between the improvised shields made of pot lids and pans and they were able to see a mountain of soda cans heading towards them like a huge wave. A truckload of drinks had overturned spilling its cargo onto the road, and the slope, together with the gale, had brought it to life in the form of a raging river. The flood of blows began literally tearing their protections out of their hands. The cans started penetrating, hitting them all over their bodies. Screams of pain were heard.

"To the bank, to the bank!" Get into the bank," Kira ordered, while trying to walk pulling the team toward the entrance of the branch that was just a few meters away. But since they were tied together it was impossible for her to move the whole group. She had to yell and give orders in a commanding voice so that the terrified citizens would come to their senses. When people panic, they become uncontrollable and do the most absurd acts, which further complicates things. Often, fear can paralyze us, freezing us, preventing us from acting. On these occasions a strong leader like the doctor, made them overcome their terror and cooperated.

They soon reached the corner entrance which was sheltered by an awning. In that nook they escaped the beating the refreshments were inflicting on them. They all entered the small corner, quite crowded. A voice was heard:

"The doors must be opened! There are survivors still out there!"

Inside the bank was a large group of people, who ran to unblock the entrance as the man wrapped in tape, holding some kitchen items against his body, had ordered them. They removed shelves and armchairs blocking the entrance and let the group in.

"Look Mom, it's the man who saved us," she said, pointing her finger at the person who had ordered them to open the entrance. The mother approached to thank him; he was a burly man, he looked like an Australian rugby league defender. They spoke briefly, since Mun-rabi-malga-frun-ragendra-chanchanawi, was a man of few words and had great difficulty holding a conversation. He was one of those people you have to extract every word from, pull them out with a corkscrew.

"By the way, what's your name?" the woman asked. There was silence, he hesitated a few moments before saying:

"You can call me Phil."

Phil is from India; his family had immigrated looking for work and trying to improve their quality of life. He worked in a family-run clothing warehouse. The textile industry needed a lot of manual labor and he started as a boy loading and unloading trucks. Partly due to genetics and also to the physical work he'd done since childhood, he had become tremendously strong. Obviously, spending the day loading and unloading merchandise didn't leave him much time to chat, hence his difficulty in relating to people.

I HAVEN'T WRITTEN ANYTHING in my diary this week. I've had some wonderful days with her. I left all my worries aside, I practically forgot about work and focused solely on her. She was the most wonderful human being on earth. She was always in a good mood, it was impossible to argue with her. Now, all those gray years were forgotten. All that distress, all those fears were erased with a smile from her mouth.

It was as if in the world there were only the two of us. I never got tired of kissing her and hugging her.

Every day at breakfast, I read the newspaper. Everything seemed like old news to me. All repeated, some I remembered as if I had just seen them. But now, I didn't want to worry about anything, I just wanted to intensely enjoy every moment.

Bubbles

IN THIS KIND OF AMNIOTIC fluid, where space and time seemed not to exist, spheres floated, moving like specks of dust in sunlight coming through a window. They resembled three-dimensional photograms, like images reflected in the balls of a Christmas tree. They were similar to small windows, small pieces of worlds, of other dimensions, of other different space-times; which somehow the machine had absorbed. Small perfect universes, captured like photographs and hermetically sealed. Their walls were not crystalline or transparent; from the inside they could not be perceived, they did not seem like enclosed spaces since the walls were a kind of space-time loop that reflected the interior like a mirror. They were even more complex than that, since they only showed the interior of the bubble, without emitting the image of people or things that were not there before the moment of capture. When walking a path that led to one of the walls of the bubble, it was reflected in such a way that it seemed to recede into an infinite horizon. Undoubtedly the most curious thing was that when anything collided against the wall, it continued without any resistance, but in the opposite direction. The same thing happened if you ran or walked forward; you touched the membrane without perceiving anything, and instantly, you changed direction, as if instead of exiting you entered. If you were alone in one of these spheres, you could die of exhaustion following a path and walking over and over in the same place without realizing it.

THE THICK GREEN GRASS reached about four inches in height. It grew on soil that for centuries had been an orchard. Now, that fertile land, which had once been carefully guarded, was left in neglect, abandoned to its fate.

How many people dedicated their lives to working that farm? What conflicts did its lease cause? How many men put those plots above all else, above themselves and their families?

A piece of black earth. Fertile at the strike of a hoe. Irrigated in sweat. Now the fruit trees that surrounded it had become wild, uprooted. Their untrimmed shoots speared green arrows in all directions.

I was in the center of that small timeless world and I felt sheltered, protected within a cathedral, within some stone ruins. Where the walls were formed by the old fruit trees, the floor carpeted by that thick, green mantle, which covered my feet and the blue sky, sprinkled with some fleeting clouds that crossed it, formed the vault. The swift passage of those cumulus clouds, meant that outside the air was blowing hard. Here the wind and even time itself seemed to stop. From those old trees new shoots sprouted. Plant beings, arms, wooden legs and sap souls. In their youth they were pampered and now, in old age, abandoned and forgotten. Old spirits that spoke with words written in the folds of their bark. Motionless observers, they have seen men pass, working and resting in the shade of their branches. Festivities and wars. Who knows? In this very place, duels, swordfights. Knights errant off the road looking for the shelter of their shade.

The sun illuminated in bursts of light, letting intermittent flashes through those fast clouds. Although it was cold outside, here the weather was warm, as if inside a greenhouse; the climate was different. I sat down and contemplated that place in silence, carefully. I listened to the sound of the wind that whistled softly as it blew through the tops of the tallest trees, poplars, white poplars. Like whispers, calm voices seemed to speak to me like spirits, souls that perhaps never left this place. I looked at the sky, gazing at the celestial vault and, leaning back, I ended up lying on the lush vegetation. The sun warmed my face and made me have to close my eyes every now and then. Each blink made it harder for me to open them and I finally fell asleep.

The Operation

SHE WAS A VERY STRONG girl, and although the prognosis was not at all encouraging, she took the doctors' diagnosis quite well.

It's incredible how one can feel healthy and strong, think they have their whole life ahead of them and, in the blink of an eye, everything falls apart. How could something like this happen? Why her? A young person, so full of life, with a great future ahead...

Where was God? Which way was He looking? What was He doing? She was a good person, why did she have to pay and not others? The righteous paying for the sinners. I wasn't a very religious person, but at times like these I felt abandoned.

She, on the other hand, was tough and thought positively, she would undergo surgery, since it was her only possibility.

"It's a very complicated operation and I'll be frank with you," the doctor said. "Even so, we can't promise you anything, since the cancer is very advanced. If we had detected it just a few months earlier, your treatment would have been not much more complicated than a simple cold."

Why does time play against us this way?

We could only enjoy two days together, and I tried to make them the most special of her life; but she didn't seem worried, she was sure she would get through this ordeal without any problems.

I've always found hospitals gloomy, with their long corridors, monochromatic decorative design. With dying people occupying the rooms, and their families waiting in the hallways. In this cold place, artificially heated, pale, where colors are unknown; I feel sick just being inside. The only warmth in that place was her gaze, always maintaining her beautiful smile.

The days seemed like months and the weeks like years. The recovery was very slow and whenever there was some improvement we always went backwards, with a new operation or an unexpected complication.

I was a complete mess; practically living in the hospital I had no time to get properly dressed and clean. But these were unimportant things, since the main thing was for her to get better as soon as possible.

Modern science has left men helpless, with nothing to be done. You feel like a lab guinea pig. Facing multitudes of tests, getting into each machine without knowing what they're doing to you. Perhaps we have lost part of our humanity by blindly trusting science. There are no more witches, sorcerers or gods left. One has no one to pray to. You feel powerless in a situation like this when a person's life depends on a machine.

I decorated her room with brightly colored flowers and also put up some posters on the walls. Making that cold place a little warmer.

When she had a good day, we talked about the old times, the good moments, the day we met thanks to my unexpected stumbling, my indecision about kissing her and the next day waiting at the library door with my stupid face. We also remembered the vacations on the coast and our bumpy honeymoon. After recalling those happy days, when I got home and found it empty I burst into tears. I tried everything humanly possible to get the best doctors and the most advanced treatments, but there was no way, it was a losing battle. I'm not someone who gives up easily, much less in a case like this one; I would fight to the end. She showed incredible strength, superhuman strength, she never faltered, she always managed to get me to smile with one of her jokes.

But there came a day when everything changed; she was fully aware that the battle was lost and decided the time had come to rest. She had earned heaven and there was no point in keeping her here in hell, suffering. I couldn't imagine life without her. I couldn't believe life was so unfair. But before I could even ponder it, I found myself attending the funeral. It was the last time I saw her; she seemed to be sleeping peacefully, with her beautiful face and dressed in her wedding dress, as she had always wanted.

Kira and the Ice Storm

SINCE I WAS A CHILD I loved reading superhero comics, people who had some supernatural power and walked the world saving others. Now movies of this kind keep appearing in theaters. Surely we all want to be like these supermen and be able to perform such fantastic feats. But the truth is we all have some power, a kind of attribute, that we tend to despise. There are those who can solve math problems in a matter of seconds, others are able to memorize phone books, there are people with all kinds of skills, although we often don't know what ours is. In most everyday situations, the most important thing is not shooting lasers from your eyes, or being able to levitate, nor breathing underwater; other various gifts are much more important, like having the courage to approach the person we love and tell them some nonsense to make them laugh. What about that superhero, the first man who was able to approach fire and master it, those anonymous people who get up very early every day and with their anonymous efforts allow us to have: light, water, bread...?

The most seriously injured kept saying meaningless things, with his muffled, barely perceptible voice. He was delirious while Kira tried to treat him. In the brokerage they had a first aid kit and the doctor made good use of it. She obtained some sedatives for the young man who remained lying on his stretcher, and also got bandages, disinfectants and dressings for the rest of her group, as everyone had various scrapes and bruises.

They were able to get comfortable, since luckily they had some old fashioned radiators, heating devices with huge blocks of stone inside. They remained on at night and the electrical resistance heated the solid block which stored the heat and slowly dissipated it throughout the day, when disconnected. For now they were hot. The bank also had emergency lights, provided with batteries that could work for twenty-four hours. A small UPS supplied power to the central computer. The security guard, who was a handyman, had disconnected it and adapted it to make the coffee machine work with its batteries. A great idea, since the machine had almost all kinds of hot liquids. The officer's walkie-talkie was on the reception desk and kept emitting noises. Samuel, an older man, in his late sixties, tall, thin, slightly hunched over, half gray half white hair, neatly combed back, hurried to grab the radio and began asking for help, pressing all the buttons, not knowing how it worked.

"Don't bother, I've been trying all day and can only get noise."

"But we need to get out of here. I have a wife and kids and they may need me."

"Calm down. The storm will pass soon, we all have relatives waiting for us. We have to keep calm."

The doctor interrupted Samuel and the guard's conversation:

"The priority is evacuating the semi-unconscious young man. I don't think he can last much longer tonight in his condition. We have to get him to a health center no matter what."

"But miss, you must be crazy! How do you expect to open an armored van?"

"Very easy: with the keys," said the guard, taking them out of his pocket.

"Then we'll wait until dawn, to see if by chance the weather improves a bit."

Kira's idea was to take the injured to a hospital as soon as possible.

"How many people can fit in the vehicle?"

"In the cabin, squeezed tight, three can fit; in the back with the patient's stretcher I don't think more than four can fit."

"Then you'll go, since you know how to drive the truck, the patient, the girl and her mother..."

And before she finished selecting them according to their survival capacity, since the doctor was choosing the weakest and sickest, Samuel jumped up furious. His pale, wrinkled complexion turned reddish.

"Who do you think you are, choosing who should leave and who has to stay?"

"Simply put, I'm selecting those with the least chance of surviving without assistance and also taking into account their physical constitution to better fit in the transport. But there's no problem, you'll go in my place."

"No! None of that," the officer interrupted, "the injured need your assistance."

When night fell, it became pitch black and they couldn't see anything through the glass. The bank's bulletproof glass storefronts withstood the blows that shook them every so often quite well. The place was quite safe and comfortable. Certainly this was not the time to try to get to the school; the most reasonable thing would be to prepare to spend the night. Once everyone warmed up, they began chatting amiably, with a cup of coffee or hot chocolate in hand. The group of eight from the bank immediately set about accommodating everyone. Sindy's mother, Barbara, kept chatting with Phil, or rather she was flirting with him. Stranger things have been seen, Kira thought, and changed her gaze to a corner where three people had gathered, the loudest and largest of them was Tim. He didn't tend to be well liked, but he had a lisping way of speaking that seemed to penetrate people's heads, getting them to do what he wanted. She had already had to confront him in the store and she really didn't like that an individual tried to manipulate others. But it seemed that two of them had forgotten that the dying young man was run over by this disturbed man. They also didn't seem to remember the argument in the shop that had nearly cost them their lives, because if they had stayed in it, by now they would be part of an ice sculpture exhibit. What might he be plotting now? She could see him ceaselessly barking orders at them and Samuel, along with another, continually nodding their heads.

The room was dimly lit, only illuminated by the small bulbs of the emergency lights. As the hours passed everyone curled up on the carpeted floor. The tables, chairs, armchairs and the like were piled at the door to reinforce the entrance, since it was the weakest point. Some were sound asleep and Tim's snoring, more like an animal than a person, could be heard. Well after midnight silence suddenly fell; then footsteps were heard, along with unusual bustling and fussing. The doctor remained lying as if she hadn't heard anything, while watching through half-open eyes. She saw the silhouette of several people sneaking from one place to another. One of them was unmistakably that stupid man again.

"What the hell are you doing?" the guard's voice broke the silence of the night. Everyone immediately woke up and some ran to see what was happening.

"Back, everybody back!" said Tim, as he waved the guard's gun in his hand and pointed it back and forth. Behind him, his two cronies with clearly distressed faces, it seemed the situation had gotten out of hand for them.

"So you were thinking of leaving us here stranded! I knew that nurse wasn't to be trusted... come on, give me the keys."

"Mr. Samuel, but you know we selected the people who need the most attention and will send a rescue team right away," said the guard.

Samuel was quite confused; suddenly he found himself overwhelmed by the situation. He didn't think Tim would explode this way. His large build gave him an air of a calm, upstanding person, but nothing could be further from the truth. As soon as he got his hands on the weapon he began threatening everyone, ceaselessly spewing all kinds of foul language, in a deep voice, spitting saliva as he spoke. He was a totally unstable person. He had gotten it in his head that Kira and the officer had planned to give an account to the police so he would be arrested for running over the young man. He would likely die any minute and they could accuse him of involuntary manslaughter. His plan was to take off with the van and leave the others there stranded. His two cronies, who didn't seem aware of his idea, now found themselves up against the ropes. On one hand, the other members they had betrayed; it wasn't very clear what Tim had put in their heads. On the other, they were now also threatened by their supposed boss.

Samuel was nervously rubbing his face with his right hand, while seeming to be plotting something. Suddenly, without warning, he pounced on Tim and began struggling to take the gun from him. Immediately the gun's owner also jumped on him, trying to subdue the deranged man and take away the revolver. The rest of the people, moved by a kind of collective rage, also threw themselves onto the men rolling on the floor. As in an American football game, a human mountain had formed on the person holding the revolver. Nothing could be seen; the women berated the criminal and scratched his face. But the guy resisted and didn't let go of the gun. A shot rang out that made everyone jump back, leaving Tim and Samuel alone.

"Criminal, you killed me!" Samuel snapped, getting to his feet with difficulty, pointing the gun at him with one hand and plugging the chest wound with the other. He aimed at Tim intending to shoot, but lowered his head to look at his chest. The white shirt was stained with blood, he brought the red-tinted hand to his face and collapsed.

Phil quickly grabbed the revolver and handed it to the guard. Kira immediately approached the deceased and put her hand on his neck to check his pulse. Her face changed instantly. She continued examining him while looking at her wristwatch to time it. Then she turned him over onto his back and, pulling on the shirt with her hands, ripped off the buttons opening it at the chest. She felt with her hands searching for the bullet hole; then she observed the red liquid dripping between her fingers and smiled. Everyone stood dumbfounded watching that scene. Barbara let go of Sindy's head, which she had been holding back until now, so she wouldn't see that crime.

Kira gave the deceased a good slap across the face and he came back to life.

"It's just mercurochrome; he had stolen a bottle and had it in his shirt pocket."

This time they gagged Tim so he wouldn't cause any more problems. Given the circumstances, the best thing was to collectively plan how to get to the school. While everyone discussed who would go in the van and which people would stay behind waiting to be rescued, the shopkeeper, Mr. Chang, carefully observed something outside, looking through the semi-frozen windows. The morning light dimly illuminated the avenue. It looked like a ghost town; ice had encrusted everything, and the wind had sculpted it, with sharp shapes that assaulted the senses. Mr. Chang looked through a crack in the frost that had come off on the other side of the glass, and took notes in his notebook. After sketching some drawings surrounded by Chinese characters, he approached the group that kept discussing who would go in the vehicle.

"But, what, what is this?" Phil blurted out.

"One second, let me see," said the officer. "No way...! The old man wants us to tie the metal booth across the street, the construction workers' shack they use while fixing the sidewalk."

"But the truck won't be able to pull it, right?"

"It sure will! I've been driving those kinds of armored vehicles all my life and you'd be surprised at the strength they have."

"But the booth doesn't have wheels..."

"That doesn't matter, its base is two steel rails it can slide on like a sled."

They got to work again to unblock the door. They were beginning to feel numb, the heaters had gone cold and they were starting to have the same problems they'd had in the store. Once the entrance was freed, they looked at each other, but no one dared go out. After a while they all looked at Phil. The man made a resigned face and prepared to leave. The procedure should be as follows: he would run to the newsstand, well to what was left of it...; from there he was only separated by a few meters from the truck. He would have to get in, start the engine following the proper steps to start it in that temperature. Once achieved, wait for it to reach sufficient heat for proper operation and then turn on the thermal diffusers to defrost the windshield. Up to that point everything seemed quite simple; then, once settled in, he would have to maneuver the vehicle toward the metal booth across the street, park in front of it, get out, grab the winch on the front of the van, pass the cable underneath and hook it to the beams forming the base of the booth. Then, he just had to drag it and stop near the bank door.

Again, the strange knight protected himself with armor taking advantage of all the office supplies they had this time. He got in a starting position, like runners at a competition. The others held onto the doors that swayed with the gusts of wind. They counted to three and opened one of the doors. Phil staggered from the shock of the air. He recovered in an instant and raced out.

It's probably happened to you before, one of those days when we've gotten up on the wrong side of the bed and everything seems to go wrong. Those days when mistakes follow one after another, leading us to put our foot in our mouths over and over? Well, this was one of those moments for Phil.

Samuel was nervously pacing in circles. He spoke aloud to himself, asking questions that only he answered. He approached the entrance, where most were holding the doors and observing the outside through the half-frozen glass.

"Let me out! I need to breathe. This air is stale, full of germs. My pulse is racing..., I think I'm having a heart attack. Of course, heart disease runs in my family and my father died of a heart attack. That's right, he was ninety-two and it hit him when he least expected it. Look, his whole life exercising, going to the gym, what for?... I don't need to exercise, I burn a lot of energy, I'm a hypochondriac. I feel a cramp in my arm, I'm sure this time it really is, it's surely a heart attack, I saw it in the Superman movie. I told my father not to train so much, but nothing, he was stubborn as a mule. Then I played a little joke on him and there, pushing up daisies... "

"But were you responsible for your father's death?"

"Well, responsible, responsible I wasn't, the coroners determined his heart failed. He was a very strange man, didn't have a very weird sense of humor. He was also the stingiest man I've ever met. He relieved himself in a bedpan and then threw it out the window, so as not to waste water flushing the toilet. His whole life working like an ant, taking all his money penny by penny to the bank. He always said that estate would be used to pay for me to get a good education, so I could go to college and yes, yes he did take me there. At sixteen I entered the university, as an assistant to load and unload trucks in the kitchen. My father leased me to an acquaintance of his for a few coins a month. Yes, that's right, in the old days children were contracted out under lease in exchange for an annual fee. Well, as I was saying, I didn't kill him, I just told him that mom had run off with a young man and taken all his savings. Honestly I didn't think he would take it so badly, he always used to play jokes on me like: I don't know who your mother slept with, because you certainly don't look like me. The older the more stupid. Everything you have big you have stupid. If you don't move out at eighteen I'll throw your things out the window and change the locks. Well those are the most affectionate phrases he ever said to me in his life. Then, it wasn't that big a deal; when I came of age he didn't throw my things out, he left my suitcase at the door... But he also had his virtues, he never drank alcohol, or smoked; well, just smoke sometimes when he found a cigarette butt on the street, and only drink water from the fountain, since you had to pay for the water at home."

"Let me out, it's an emergency!"

They had to hold him down and put a bag on his head again so he wouldn't hyperventilate and could calm down again. And he thought I was weird! (I put the text in italics myself).

I HAD A NIGHTMARE TONIGHT; I got up pale and trembling. She was sleeping peacefully. I went to the kitchen and made linden tea. I sat down in the dining room, trying to forget that old feeling. My mouth tasted like iron, and my tongue was so dry it felt like cardboard. Old ghosts returned to my mind, reminding me of all those bad times.

It was clear I couldn't forget them, nor ignore them, so I would have to face them head on.

After all I had been through, this wasn't the time to waver. The best thing was to relax, lie down again and try to fall asleep. In the morning, once rested, with clearer ideas I would think about how to solve the problem.

"HOW'S IT GOING? GOOD morning. This bubble seems comfortable, but you shouldn't have fallen asleep. You have to be very careful. I always sleep with one eye open. You can call me Alb," said the white-haired old man as he held out his hand to Agnux, greeting him and at the same time helping him get up.

"Agnux, my name is Agnux."

"Very good Agnux. How long have you been here? What a stupid question. Let me ask you instead: how many bubbles have you gone through?"

"Bubbles?"

"Yes, bubbles, spheres, worlds or whatever you want to call them."

"I don't understand you."

"So you're new here. Don't worry, son, it will take you some time. So it's still operating..."

His voice was powerful, authoritative, like a general's, and at the same time soft and sweet. It had a touch, a kind of accent, I'd say northern. He was an elderly man, but difficult to gauge, since although his hair was white and his face marked by the passage of time, he radiated the same vitality as a 15 year old boy.

The man wouldn't stop talking, he seemed to enjoy the conversation, as if he hadn't spoken to anyone in a long time.

"What year is it up there? How are things going? Have the Americans and Soviets launched any bombs yet?"

"I don't know what's wrong with me, I feel confused."

"Oh yes! I forgot. Don't worry. You're in a kind of post-traumatic state, but little by little you'll remember. It took me quite a while to realize my situation, plus I didn't have as much luck with my first bubble. From the very beginning, I found myself with those kinds of hellish worm-like creatures."

My head was spinning, I didn't understand anything at all. I don't know if all this was a dream, because I couldn't find any logic in it. I slapped my pants at calf height, as if brushing off grass blades that had adhered, but more energetically, without it looking like an artificial movement, but with the aim of feeling the blows on my legs, thus confirming that I wasn't dreaming.

Alb sat down and contemplated the magnificent landscape. He seemed to meditate like a Buddhist monk. For a few minutes there was absolute silence, then the man looked at me and said:

"Now that you'll be a little more clear-headed, I'll explain where we are. I'll tell it to you in the simplest way so you can understand me, but you'll have to fit the pieces together over time and discover the details. If I were to tell you everything you wouldn't accept it as true and in any case this isn't the time or place. It would be a complete waste of time.

If you don't understand something, son, don't worry, you will later."

"Well, we're inside a sphere, a space-time singularity, a piece of some place on earth that has been, to put it simply, transported to another dimension. The bubbles are like residual photographs that the machine absorbed when the time bridge opened. An Einstein-Rosen bridge, more commonly called a wormhole, a tunnel opened in the very fabric of the universe, capable of connecting different eras, places and dimensions. The machine was activated in the forties, when we were conducting an experiment with huge electromagnets, which was meant to absorb radar signals, thus providing us invisibility from the enemy. Some of the scientists working with me disappeared after being sucked in by it; I kept working from that day onward in order to bring those people back. Several young, brilliant researchers with promising futures had been condemned to a prison for centuries and centuries, until the end of time. I swore to work tirelessly doing whatever was necessary to be able to bring my old colleagues back home. Unfortunately I overlooked something in my mathematical equations. I made calculations for decades, worked tirelessly, totally abstracting myself from the world around me. Many of my colleagues thought I had lost my mind, that I was no longer the brilliant scientist of yesteryear. But the whole project was top secret and we couldn't speak about what had happened; plus I had no time or desire to explain something they possibly would never understand anyway. It took me a lifetime to do the equations needed to solve the wormhole's instability problem. I needed to amplify that signal and modulate it correctly so the bridge would stay open long enough to get my old companions out of their spherical prisons."

On April 18, 1955 I entered the parameters into the machine which had remained on up to that date, in an old government-owned basement. The tunnel remained stable, but as I told you, something my equations didn't account for came into play. The hole became large, the size and shape of a subway tunnel. The feeling was like finding myself on the platform looking into the darkness, waiting for the train lights to appear at any moment. The whole old basement fell silent, time seemed to stop. Then an unbearable sound, screams, shrieks that couldn't be human, made me crouch down covering my ears with my palms. A kind of black objects, leaves, sticks, stones, were spat out from the hole, hitting me all over my body, scratching my face. Then, silence took over the room, the clock seemed to stop again; but this time I sensed that something had changed, something was wrong. I had an uneasy feeling, I felt the presence of an intelligent being that didn't belong to this world. I immediately turned around and I could see a dark figure, a silhouette like a man's, but deep in my heart I knew it wasn't human. I felt as if ancient legends, ancestral beliefs, childhood fears, had materialized in that being. It was exiled evil, a diabolical being, the devil who had escaped from hell itself. A being older than any religion or culture, older than the human race itself, even older than our own earth, solar system or world.

It moved slowly, approaching me; I was able to see that the being's body was formed by a tangle of black worms that all moved together.

Although it had a human appearance, in reality its whole body was made up of a mountain of black worms. It wasn't a single organism. Of course it wasn't the kind of devil or demon I had always imagined. I always thought of the devil as a kind of man, which raised me many questions. Since if it was a person, an intelligent being who had been there since the beginning of time, who knew the origin of life on earth and even much more, there would be some way to talk to him. Such an ancient being with so much knowledge by force had to be a rational being. He could tell me the origin of his anger, why he maintained that eternal struggle. I even went much further in my approaches: if he was immortal, he would know the origin of the universe, and if so, how could he be the representative of evil in the entire universe, it being infinite; because if there were parallel infinite universes and in each of them infinite systems, galaxies and worlds similar to ours, he would have competitors, Martian devils green in color and with antennas. The confusion increased as I added more variables. One thing was clear: if I met a being of this kind, no matter what he did to me, I wouldn't stop asking him questions. Well, all this was forgotten when I realized that ancient being, that black, dark and foul being described by so many religions, was an organism made up of some kind of worms. It was only like a virus; there was nothing human about it, only a being that spread like the plague, like cancer, for the sole purpose of assimilating what surrounded it, feeding and reproducing.

After finishing that astonishing story he went on: Look there's our exit, right behind that old fig tree.

Now that he had said it, looking more closely at that point, you could see a kind of distortion, like a blurry stain occupying the place, similar to an out of focus photograph. We set off, although I felt very comfortable in that place. We went through the vegetation tangle and Alb entered, immediately disappearing.

"Come on! What are you waiting for?"

I heard his voice in the distance.

THE DOMINO EFFECT CONTINUED knocking down one pawn after another. The freezing wind collided with the humid air below, turning it into solid ice. Instantly everything was covered by a crystalline layer. The pavement became a skating rink, preventing traffic, whether vehicles or pedestrians. People were isolated in their homes. Those who were outside would be very lucky if they managed to reach some shelter before being injured from inevitable slides, or being hit by falling tree branches collapsing under the weight of the accumulated ice. On one side and another you could hear that resounding sound of breaking glass produced by the crystallized trees shattering against the ground. The wind seemed to burn the skin. It was cutting, well-honed blades that shredded your body on contact. It wasn't possible to survive for long outside. Clothes became impregnated by sheet after sheet, making them heavy and stiff.

At home one could take shelter from the storm. At least that's how it seemed at first. But soon the refuge provided by our homes was transformed into a deadly trap. Homes built with thin layers of material couldn't retain heat inside. But no one ever worried about that, since that's what the electrical and gas networks were for, which fed energy to the heaters. Of course no one thought that service could easily be interrupted, turning those pretty little houses into real freezers.

Everything began to come together, like a plan concocted by a brilliant mind in the service of evil. Chance, or rather the ignorance of those who designed our cities, chained one problem after another. Homes were totally dependent on the energy produced at power plants miles away. This stopped arriving, first in some isolated residences, which had their supply cut off by falling branches that tore down the low voltage cables, which hung from facade to facade crossing from one side of the street to the other, carrying electricity from one place to another, in a chaotic manner, without any kind of planning. In the same way that Edison put light bulbs on one side and another to light up his workshop and surroundings, in that way, we continued stringing cables, connecting them to each other, without any plan or blueprint, until forming a huge tangled mess that brought light to the whole world.

These initially isolated cases kept emergency services busy with repairs. Calls overwhelmed switchboards, then everything went off. Users were left without communication. Telephones didn't work, electricity and gas didn't arrive. The whole system had been knocked down. The huge pylons that transported energy from the power plants had been toppled by the weight of the ice accumulated on the cables. They lay on the white ground, like defeated giants kneeling.

HE WORE A CLASSICALLY cut suit, you could even say an old-fashioned style, with vest and pocket watch, which gave him a Victorian air. If it weren't for his marked accent, the clothing, you'd say he was English. He had long, disheveled white hair. His thick mustache was the same color. His slightly sunken eyes accentuated his penetrating gaze.

He really seemed very familiar to me. I think he reminded me of an actor, he bore a certain resemblance to Sean Connery.

AT FIRST, IT HARDLY seemed important, you could even fall asleep, but after spending a whole day with your body imprisoned in a straitjacket and your head stuffed in a cloth sack, you completely lost track of time and thought you'd never see the light of day again. After the first hours of uncertainty, panic took over; screams, sobs and the salty taste of tears kept you company in the following hours. The amazing thing came much later; when you hit rock bottom like Dante there wasn't even a shred of fear left; from that moment an external force was perceived in the form of enveloping heat.

The punishment cell was hardly more spacious than the inside of a closet. A light bulb that was always on the verge of burning out dimly lit the tiny room. The light was always on, but if the one who put you in the cell was Fat Tim, you knew that although the room was always lit, it wouldn't do you any good, since he loved covering inmates heads with a bag he'd tie around your neck with a cord. The fat man enjoyed terrorizing the patients at the psychiatric hospital and if you didn't show any signs of panic, he'd start shaking you while shouting threats.

It seems the thin line separating sanity from insanity isn't very well defined and, depending on who judges you or simple chance, one could be the sick person or the nurse.

We only went outside on rare occasions, so all the inmates had a pale, dull, pasty white complexion. The days passed without any difference, disappearing without leaving a trace like water escaping through your hands. I felt as if I were watching the world change aboard a time machine. Things changed around me over the years, everything was transformed; where there was once an empty room with nothing more one day a piece of furniture appeared, a white table matching the rest of the sanatorium's equipment. After that, chairs, and then more tables, then paper and pencils; quickly, in one corner a cabinet appeared, a corner cabinet and later a TV; we spent all day in front of it. The years flew by at the speed of shooting stars. Surprisingly, one day, upon looking at the once white walls, I now saw colored paint; color seemed contagious since when I looked at the tables, I was stunned to see their different colors. Everything filled with color; even the old TV was replaced with a new color one. We no longer spent as much time inside and went out to the garden every sunny day. So finally even our faces ended up coloring.

The center's staff kept changing and with the recent hired nurses new treatments arrived, based on modern therapies; but Fat Tim was still on staff and kept torturing patients whenever possible.

Times changed so much that we were even allowed to celebrate our birthdays with cake and candles. It was Hot Coal's birthday, and like everyone else his was celebrated with a cake. It was a huge cake that would yield portions for everyone. The cake had little colored candles, as many years old as he was.

"Please, please! Can I? Can I?" said Hot Coal, pointing to the matchbox intending to reach for it. Fat Tim raised his heavy hand over Hot Coal's head fully intending to give him a good slap, but he had to instantly change his threatening demeanor to a nicer one since he was being watched by one of the new lady doctors. So much to his chagrin he had to watch as Hot Coal lit the birthday cake candles. He held the lit match, staring fixedly at the flame and stood still for a few moments, hypnotized by the glow of the flame; just when everyone was starting to get nervous he reacted and lit the cake candles as if nothing had happened.

Without anyone noticing he managed to pocket some matches in his pants pocket. He hid them for days waiting for the right time to light them; Sunday morning, during the children's movie they were forced to attend like a liturgical act, he lit one of the matches and held it to the curtains at the back of the room. Fat Tim, along with the rest of the nurses and caregivers were in the front row laughing loudly at the old movie. By the time they realized, the whole room was up in flames and panic broke out. Some ran to put out the fires, others to call the fire department and taking advantage of the chaos and open doors, Pasca advanced, reaching the visiting room and finally the reception. The inmate walked in a strange way, hopping on some tiles and avoiding others. But no one noticed that he was getting closer and closer to the exit. The firefighters burst in charging down the main corridor and the sick man went outside. He kept walking in that peculiar way, as if walking, jumping and dancing at the same time to music only he could hear. He crossed the garden, which he had rarely been taken to, and a little beyond the huge gate with its spear-shaped steel doors. The whole path was clear; so he continued down the white gravel path that invited him to leave the place.

"Wait a minute: Has anyone seen Hot Coal?" the fat man asked, but no one answered him. He ran looking for him throughout the sanatorium, but didn't find a trace of him. Then he looked out the second floor window, the one facing the street, and was petrified, mouth agape. The patient was escaping by taking those strange steps down the road. He ran downstairs as fast as he could; he didn't want to look ridiculous in front of the sanatorium director, having to explain the fire and how an inmate had escaped. He went down to the courtyard and arrived at the employee parking lot.

"Shit, damn it!" he muttered as he felt his pants pockets looking for his car keys. He had left them in his street clothes, in the men's locker room. He ran through the hallways again pushing the people fleeing the smoke.

"Good, I've got them!"

He grabbed the keys, and took off running again for the vehicle. He got in, inserted the key in the ignition and it started right up. He tore out, the gravel from the driveway spit out by the tires. He drove down the road at full speed and, just like that, something hit the windshield, leaving a mark on the glass; then a hail storm the size of fists began. They were pieces of ice the size of tomatoes. Visibility was nearly zero and at the speed he was going, he entered the city bumping around. He lost control of the car, he tried stopping it, but it wouldn't respond. In the midst of that, cars began crashing into each other, traffic accidents caused chaos everywhere. When he was barely managing to reduce speed and gain control, he saw Pasca with his clumsy gait. He turned the corner and lost sight of him; then he slammed the gas pedal to the floor; he was willing to take him back dead or alive. But when he entered the intersection at such high speed and the icy road, he began skidding. He jerked the wheel to the right; then corrected to the left but was unable to stay on the path he wanted. And when he realized it, he was up on the sidewalk.

The accumulated hail on the ground formed a solid layer several centimeters thick; this turned streets into skating rinks. A car turned the corner, driving too fast for the conditions. Its windows were cracked from the storm and you couldn't quite see who was driving. It approached at high speed toward the door of the shop where there were still many people. It tried to turn right, but the tires lost traction and it kept moving while spinning. At the moment Kira said watch out, the SUV plowed into the pedestrians. Screams were heard and she ran over to see what happened. Between several people they picked up an individual who was under the vehicle. Others berated the driver, pounding on the bodywork. Fearing he would get lynched, the driver engaged the locks. He was a middle-aged, obese, very pale-skinned man dotted with freckles.

On the ground lay an unconscious young man due to the injuries sustained in the collision.

"He killed him!"

PHIL RAN LIKE A CHILD trying to catch a chicken, half crawling half on foot, making more S's than a drunk. The storm didn't allow him to do anything else. Finally, after endless minutes, he managed to reach the newsstand and take refuge leaning on the structure that was still standing. A few more meters ahead was the truck. After a few seconds to catch his breath, he raced out again. The sidewalk, which from that point on was made of shiny little tiles that looked more like bathroom tiles, was as slippery as an ice rink. And there goes our first contestant, Phil, thirty-seven years old, with a psychedelic homemade office worker costume. He does a spin, jumps, and another, rolls down the street and performs a splendid choreography that seems improvised on the go. He manages to grab onto a lamppost; even though he banged his crotch, he keeps going, no pain... He heads back to the van, it seems he still has an ace up his sleeve, one last trick and yes, he delights us again with another one of his masterful skating performances.

Well, the truth is the situation was no laughing matter, but what could they do, cry?

On the third try he finally managed to grab onto the bumper of the vehicle; then he searched for the keys in his pocket, but nothing, he couldn't find anything. He looked at the sidewalk where he had rolled so many times and, indeed, there they were, dropped in the middle. The gusts of wind dragged them. Images flashed through his mind of how the keys would disappear going down the avenue. That kind of thing that tends to happen when a piece of paper slips out of your hand, and just when you try to pick it up off the floor, the wind moves it, forcing you to run after it. He didn't think twice and threw himself back onto the ice rink. Just when he almost had them within reach they started moving, but diving onto the pavement, he managed to get hold of them. Even under those horrible conditions, with his hands and face frozen, with the cold wind penetrating chilling him to the bone, even with the pain from the blows he had taken, he let out a tremendous laugh. He walked back to the armored vehicle, opened the door and began pressing the buttons that activated the starter and cold start system. It was a vehicle prepared for all kinds of conditions and its cabin resembled an airplane's more than a car's, buttons, indicators and switches, filled the interior even on the ceiling. He had memorized the sequence to start the engine under those circumstances. The truth is, the officer should have been the one to perform this operation, but if you could see his build and physical condition, you'd know why no one voted for him to be the one assigned. The diet of doughnuts and coffee gave him a life preserver waistline. The man selected was certainly the most suitable for such a mission. He managed to start the truck and after a few minutes, the heating system defrosted the windows and managed to warm up Phil, who up to that point had remained rubbing his frozen limbs and putting them where they call "the poor man's heater" by sticking your hands in your crotch to warm them up.

What followed was not easy at all. He put it in first to move the van and reach the metal container. But the jalopy didn't budge; the tires spun on the icy asphalt. He heard voices. From the branch everyone shouted to him and gestured with their hands. But what the hell was going on? He wondered, shrugging his shoulders. What the hell were they trying to tell him? As if a light bulb went on in his head, he remembered he had to activate the four wheel drive lever. Once this little mishap was overcome, the vehicle moved easily over the ice. He backed up, to stick the truck to the sheet metal booth, took a deep breath preparing to jump outside and tie the cable to the trailer. He thought twice about it and finally forced himself to go out saying aloud:

"Come on, let's go, let's go."

Once again he found himself braving the storm. Clinging to the bodywork, he reached the front and grabbed the shackle protruding from the winch. He pulled with all his might and managed to pull out several meters of cable. He passed it under the wheels, not without difficulty and then, once in the back, he just had a few centimeters left to connect it. He was pulling with all his might, his whole body trembled due to the muscular tension, but he couldn't reach to connect it.

"He won't make it! No, there's nothing to be done. Someone go out and help him!" Samuel shouted without removing the bag from his face, getting ready to rush out. But no one flinched, they completely ignored him.

"Mmmm! Come on, a little more..." he murmured, squeezing his teeth as he pulled with all his might on the cable. There was a click and the hook attached firmly to the steel beam.

The rest was a piece of cake. He drove the transport to the doors of the brokerage. The tons of metal creaked and crackled as it dragged along the road. The vehicle had plenty of horsepower for any kind of emergency that might arise. The trailer slid better than expected; if it weren't for the havoc it was wreaking on the asphalt, leaving some good furrows in its path, it could be a good means of transportation. A few meters down the street they encountered the first difficulty. Some crashed cars completely blocked the avenue. Eight vehicles lay joined together cutting off the passage.

"Now what?"

"Don't worry, now you'll see what this monster can do."

The driver knew very well what kind of machine he was driving. The wedge-shaped, forged steel snout was designed for these types of situations. In movies a car usually blocks the armored truck's path and it has to stop, when the thieves take the opportunity to rob it; but in reality, these transports are designed to plow through anything that gets in their way.

"Hold on tight!" he shouted over the intercom hanging from the ceiling, connected to a coiled cord, holding it with one hand to press the transmitter button and using the other to maneuver the steering wheel, driving the van toward the weakest point in the barricade. The passengers heard the warning and quickly held on wherever they could. Indeed, the vehicle pushed the cars aside thanks to the shape of its snout and they continued on without any more trouble.

"Did you see that?" he commented to Phil as he drove, eyes fixed on the road.

"Yeah, what a ride, how we plowed through that pile of cars."

"No, I don't mean that, I mean did you notice everything."

"I don't know what you mean."

"Look, since yesterday morning I haven't seen any other people besides those of us in this group. There's no one in the cars, not even corpses. There's also no one in the houses, nor can anyone be heard anywhere. The radio doesn't work either."

"But we heard the emergency instructions to follow on the radio."

"Yes, but the announcement was a recording, it wasn't a live broadcast. I also got it on my radio and listened to the same thing for hours."

"I don't know where you're going with this."

"I mean something very strange is happening here. I wouldn't be surprised if there had been an accident at the nuclear plant on the outskirts of the city."

"But that wouldn't explain the disappearance of the bodies."

"I don't know, I read a news story once about some nuclear plant workers who had disappeared. Apparently the radiation was able to dissolve their bodies."

"But then how is it that we're still alive?"

"I have no idea, but what I am sure of is that something very strange is going on here."

"We should mention it to the others, surely the doctor can tell us something..."

"I think for now it's better not to say anything, it could cause panic. We'll have time to talk to the doctor alone once we get to the school.

There have to be more survivors there, everyone knows it's the meeting place in case of any catastrophe."

The convoy advanced down the middle of the promenade, clearing a path through the multitude of vehicles, junk and debris populating the street. Everything seemed to be going smoothly; at the rate they were progressing they would reach the meeting point in a matter of minutes.

"Brake!"

The officer slammed on the brakes and the armored vehicle began sliding uncontrollably. The avenue was blocked by a huge ditch. The ground had sunk some thirty meters. Perhaps an underground tunnel collapsed and the earth gave way. The transport slid on the frozen surface and if they didn't do something soon they would end up in that pit. The driver had to think fast, and seeing the cargo they were carrying he knew he wouldn't be able to brake in time. He released the brake and traced as wide a curve as he could, skirting the ravine. The trailer with all the other team members slid across; it continued with half the base on the asphalt and the other half in the air at the height of a tenth floor. It managed to stay half airborne thanks to the enormous weight of the truck holding it by one corner. When they crossed the street, they abruptly ended the ride crashing into a building's wall. The convoy literally entered all the way into the kitchen.

"You okay?"

"Where did you get your license?" Phil joked, which reassured the driver, who quickly radioed the passengers in the container. But no one answered. The two men looked at each other worriedly and he tried to communicate with the rest of the companions again. The radio only picked up static. Suddenly someone knocked on the driver's window.

"God, what a scare!"

He opened the door and Kira yelled at them:

"Are you crazy? We almost got killed back here."

They didn't realize how close they had come to dying. If they had seen how they flew over the precipice...!

"Is everyone okay?"

"Fortunately yes, we just have a few bruises."

Then they told him what happened. They all got out of the transport and discussed the situation and the new plan to follow to get to the destination.

"Let's see; on the map we are here, at this point. Just two blocks away from the school. But to get there on foot we'd have to go out there, where we wouldn't last long under the storm. Plus, the avenue is blocked and we'd have to go up and cross Swan Street and then go down 42nd."

"Wait a minute, wait a minute, that's impossible..."

I preferred not to transcribe Samuel's dialogues since they are depressingly cringeworthy.

Once again Mr. Chang broke away from the group and began observing and taking notes in his notebook. After a while he approached the group again, which was in the midst of discussion. Tim remained gagged, sitting on the floor and, although his mouth was taped shut, he constantly interrupted by producing a kind of nasal mooing. On the other hand, the hypochondriac breathed into his bag and expounded his theories on evolution. The rest of the group discussed the way to get to the evacuation point in a reasonable manner. He wedged himself into the middle of the group showing his little notebook.

"I can't believe I didn't think of it!" the guard exclaimed. Apparently he was the only one who understood the shopkeeper's strange drawings in his notebook.

"This man's a genius! We can take a shortcut through the inside of the building; these buildings have long hallways and we'll only have to open up some holes in certain partitions to continue on our way. That way we'll be sheltered from the storm."

AS USUAL, THE FIRST thing I did was have breakfast and go over the news. I perfectly remembered one of the news items talking about a new biodiesel extracted from trash; it was the day of the domestic incident. The pan she had put on the stove to make some crepes would be left forgotten causing a small kitchen fire. Although the fire wasn't very big the amount of smoke alarmed the entire neighborhood.

Just as she was leaving the kitchen, I hurried to enter it. The pan would have only been on the fire for a few seconds and I could avoid the incident.

I grabbed the still cold pan by the black Teflon handle and removed it from the stove. But as soon as I left it in the sink, it caught fire. I dropped it in fright, with such bad luck that it fell next to the kitchen towel roll, which immediately burned, producing a large cloud of smoke. She arrived frightened in the kitchen and, although the emergency was already under control, we had to go out into the street poisoned by the smoke. The alarmed neighbors asked us what had happened. It was exactly the same situation experienced in the past. Only my actions had changed, but the result was exactly the same.

THEY HAD BEEN WALKING nonstop for about two hours; they had retraced their steps several times, but couldn't find the exit. The flashlight was starting to lose power.

"We should have listened to the bricklayer; I'm tired of having you as a partner, I keep having to eat all your crap.

"If you weren't happy with my decision you should have taken the other path! I'm absolutely sure it's this way."

"That's what you've said already like five times in the last hour and the only thing that's for sure here is that we're lost and we're going to be the laughingstock of the whole police station. They'll be making fun of us until retirement day."

"We both have the same rank and no one forced you to follow me..."

At that point in the argument the light went out and they were left in total darkness. It didn't take them long to take different paths. Sebastian chose to take the upward path, he thought it was the most logical if he wanted to find the exit. But after walking a long stretch the ascent stopped and the gallery now extended over flat ground. Later it began descending; after the distance he had walked it seemed better to keep going; wherever it led, the underground had to lead somewhere. He lost track of time and when he stopped for an instant, he noticed the sound of footsteps behind him; unconsciously he had been ignoring them because they seemed like the echo of his own footsteps. Then, as he walked the noises started up again.

"Sir, is that you?"

He thought the bricklayer must be wandering around lost too, because he perfectly recognized the sound of his partner's footsteps and these were clearly different. A few seconds passed and no one answered his questions. He quickened his pace and his pursuer also increased speed. He then began to run and could hear something approaching him faster and faster. He tripped on something in the middle of the floor and hit the ground hard. The pain was so intense that for a moment he forgot about his pursuer. He remembered he had a lighter in his jacket pocket. It was a souvenir lighter that he never used. He took it out of his pocket and spun the wheel that produced sparks against the flint. His leg hurt enormously and his side too; due to the tremendous suffering it was very difficult for him to breathe, surely he had some broken ribs. He couldn't get the flame to ignite and the little sparks briefly lit up the place like a camera flash. He was able to see a lump at his feet, but didn't have time to see what it was; he clicked the lighter again and was able to see his partner's body lying on the floor. The pain kept increasing and when he examined his leg he could feel the broken bone.

"Who's there? Is that you?" he asked toward where the breathing was coming from, but no one answered him. He pulled out his gun as quickly as he could and aimed at that area.

The silence was interrupted by gunshots; you could see how the cavern lit up in the distance by fleeting flashes.

"Help! Help!"

I REMEMBER THE MOIST earth giving off heat, as after a summer storm. The walls of granite stone formed by perfect cubes chiseled by chisel, besieged the precinct, forming an irregular perimeter. From the same carved rock, ghostly figures emerged representing Templar knights, unrelenting ever-vigilant guardians. With their stone helmets, breastplates and swords, they guarded that place. There were a dozen, firm, looking straight ahead with their cruciform broadswords with their tips resting on the ground, one hand on top of the other on the final piece of the hilt. Their height was imposing, and their realism was such that they seemed like real fossilized soldiers. The walls curved inward in a vaulted shape covering that entire space with the dome. The light came from above, entering through openings perfectly made in the ceiling. Moonlight entered through the cracks directing its rays at the statues. The rest of the place remained in shadows.

I heard a sound behind me, but when I turned around I didn't see anything. I heard something again; I paid more attention to it and the hair on my body began to stand on end. A ghostly voice, a phantom breath, seemed to approach me from behind. I tensed up, stiff as a board and squeezed my eyes shut tight. I wanted to disappear, become invisible in the face of that threat. I waited for something to grab me from behind, but nothing happened. I kept hearing the sound loudly; once again I turned trying to see the being producing it. But there was nothing, which made my heart skip a beat as that breathing grew louder. The statues seemed to be watching my movements. I strained to see in the dark and made out a shape on the ground, something big undefined. The first thing I thought was to start running, but my legs didn't respond, and anyway there was nowhere to go. After contemplating that dark lump for a few seconds, I decided to approach to see what it was. More afraid than ashamed, I slowly inched closer.

With each step the silhouette looked more like a being lying on the floor. Already just meters away I called out.

"Hey!"

"I'm coming, I'm coming, where's that damn alarm clock. Oh! Son, it's you. It seems I fell asleep upon entering this bubble.

I had never been so happy to see someone. It was Alb with his calm, serene manner, with his peculiar accent and very polite way of speaking.

Once he had woken up, we began searching the place for an exit. The enclosure seemed completely airtight. We couldn't find a door, a trapdoor, not even a crack in the construction. The cobblestones had been placed with such meticulousness that not even a hair fit between them.

"This place, the shape of the statues, the type of building, reminds me when I studied the history of Freemasonry. They always hid everything behind secret passages, subtly camouflaged so that only an alert mind could find the key. Let's observe the place well: there are twelve guardians. Like there are twelve months in a year, if you look there are four groups, each made up of three of the statues, and differentiated by the symbols on their shields, which surely symbolize the four seasons. Deducing this, that one over there must be January and as it's the first month..."

We examined the statue more closely and found a subtle difference from the rest. Its eyes, carved out of white stone, unlike the other figures that looked straight ahead, this one looked at its right arm, which rested on the weapon.

"I think... surely if... I've got it!"

He managed to activate a mechanism that immediately opened a passage behind the statue.

HE WALKED ALONG THE edge of the clearing with his head down looking back and forth as if he had lost something. To the right and left the grounds were planted with stones; such a quantity formed a mantle looking like a potato patch. Pasca kept watching the number of shapes and colors. Something caught his curiosity and he headed with clumsy steps over the cobbled plot toward that object.

Pasca was only six years old and while his parents worked in the fields, he usually wandered around the surroundings, looking for small smooth pebbles that he kept in a wooden drawer, buried behind his house as if it were treasure.

He approached the artifact and examined it in detail; then he passed his small hands over its metallic surface, feeling its entire contour until finding a notch. He got back on his feet and took a string out of his pants pocket; it was a plant fiber cord, and passing one end through the groove he tied it to the strange object. He spent the whole day walking from one place to another, dragging the heavy metal artifact as if it were a dog on a leash.

"Who's that kid?" one of the boys asked.

"I think his name's Pasca, he's the son of the farm workers."

"Come here shorty, we want to talk to you."

The child stopped when he heard these words, and for a moment considered his possibilities of escape; although he was a little slow for his age, he immediately knew those boys didn't have good intentions. If he took off running they would catch him right away, and after making them run the reprisals would surely be worse. So after hesitating for some time, he approached them.

"What's the matter kid, weren't you thinking of running away?" said one of the teenagers, and without allowing time for a word, grabbed Pasca by the ears so hard he nearly lifted him off the ground. The child didn't let out a whimper. He had gone through this situation before and knew the boys exercising the law of the strongest would subject him to their mistreatment until they tired of it. Knowing his parents, his mother's protection was on the other side of the hill rising before his eyes, only aggravated the feeling of helplessness. After shaking and insulting him to their heart's content, they thought of something new to continue having fun with the little boy. They tied and gagged him to a tree. A few inches from his feet they piled up branches, forming a good pile, and when they finished one of the kids said:

"We're going to roast you like a turkey at Christmas."

"Wait a minute, first I want to make him confess."

"Confess? What does he have to confess?"

"Well that he's a witch, idiot!"

They prepared another pile of firewood a little further away; as soon as they finished, one of the boys took three matches out of his pants pocket. He got ready to light the fire, placing a flat rock next to him and rubbing the matchhead on the rough surface of the stone.

"Shit!" he exclaimed when he saw the flammable tip had worn off without even producing a spark. Now there were only two left and this uncomfortable the boy a bit. Pasca watched the second match intently as the brat rubbed it against the cobblestone surface, hoping it wouldn't light either.

"Damn it!" he shouted when he saw the second one hadn't lit either.

Pasca exhaled, releasing air after seeing the second match didn't light either. Now there was certain worry on the boy's face, as he held the last match in his hand. Apparently, having carried them loose in his pocket for so long had dampened them and now they were useless. He brought the last one to the flat flint surface. The little boy held his breath again, wishing with all his might that the match wouldn't light. The boy rubbed it gently to keep the head from coming off, he frictioned it several times each time faster, but the wooden body was starting to lose its phosphorous coating and had barely produced some sparks. Driven by desperation he rubbed the stick faster and faster and although there was barely anything combustible material left, it finally ignited. The anguish could be seen on Pasca's face, although what could still happen was that the freshly gathered branches forming the piles of firewood wouldn't catch fire. He brought the small flame close, protecting it with his palm so the breeze wouldn't blow it out, and as soon as the flame touched the bark of the branches they caught fire.

The situation was precarious and seemed to lead to tragedy. The boys began passing the ember that ignited on the ends of their sticks near his face. The child became so afraid that he wet his pants. The poor child cried in terror, which seemed to fill his tormentors with satisfaction. When bringing the burning tip of a stake close became boring, they began putting the searing tips of their sticks on the child's soft skin, they burned his hands while the little one wouldn't stop crying.

"Look! What's he got in that hand?"

"Looks like a rope."

"I already know that dummy; I mean what's on the other side of the rope."

Pasca still had that strange object he had found on the ground with him.

The boys stopped torturing him and became interested in that unusual artifact. They handled it trying to figure out what it was; then they smashed it against a rock to try to open it and see what was inside, but when they didn't manage it they ended up losing interest in the object and focused again on the little boy.

"Your time has come witch and you will die in the flames!" said one of the boys and with a branch taken from the first fire, he prepared to light the pile of firewood stacked by the child's feet.

"Wait, one second!" said the boy who seemed to be in charge.

"Let's burn that thing first, so he can see what's going to happen to him."

They put the object on the flames while it turned red due to the high temperature; they hurled frightening phrases at little Pasca.

He knew the end was near and wouldn't stop sobbing.

A blinding light illuminated everything, the sound of a hundred thunderclaps exploded in his ears and then he could only hear a high-pitched ringing. Everything slowed down and frame by frame he saw how the air filled with a cloud of fire, making him close his eyes; when he opened them again no one was there, the teenagers had vaporized, the fire had swallowed them up. The huge explosion drew the farm workers and they rescued Pasca. The child was never the same again; after the incident a sick fascination with fire grew day by day inside him.

Agnux tonight I dreamed of her again

I WOKE UP WITH A START. My body was drenched in sweat and my head was spinning. I tried to calm down, but my heart was beating so hard it hurt my chest. I knew it was just a new hallucination, but I couldn't get past that suffocating pain. I often dreamed of her, but what began as a peaceful dream, abruptly ended like a nightmare. We danced embraced, spinning around and around. As everything spun around me, I looked into her eyes and couldn't stop smiling at her. The feeling was real, so real it couldn't be differentiated from any of the memories I had of her. But like a sunset, like a candle as it's consumed, the darkness lunged at us. I held her tight, so nothing could separate her from my arms. I embraced her against me, but she disappeared transforming into smoke, hitting me like the wind hiding around the corner.

WE WALKED DOWNHILL along the dry riverbed. It was a unique place; on both sides the dense tangled vegetation climbed to the mountaintops. Certainly, the best path was the one the stream marked, although it wasn't without difficulties. The terrain was made up of white stones, like marble, rounded and polished, some barely two centimeters and others enormous like a house. Progress was slow and laborious; walking on the small stones constantly made me lose my balance. They weren't well seated on the base, and when you stepped on them they moved. The worst thing was that some turned into angry animals and kicked at my ankles. I tried to continue on the larger rocks, jumping from one to another; this took a long time having to zigzag. The air was fresh, clean mountain air. The wind didn't blow and the temperature was good. After walking nonstop for a while, I looked back and saw how the white gravel path was lost in infinity. I had walked much further than it seemed to me. Walking downhill is much more rewarding. The sky was a brilliant blue and the sun shone in the center. The place looked like it was taken from one of my dreams; the only thing that worried me was knowing where the water had gone... Could it have evaporated? Was it simply due to drought? But the vegetation was tall and green. A fleeting fear crossed my mind: Was there a dam upstream holding back all the water?

We continued on our way at a livelier pace due to my fears which, apparently, Alb also shared. I always tried to look back, checking the streambed out of the corner of my eye. I imagined a gigantic wave could appear at any moment sweeping everything away. Focused on the descent and my water paranoia, I didn't pay attention to the wooden constructions that could be seen from time to time. Finally, a huge wheel, like those of watermills, caught my attention. We approached to observe that enormous structure in more detail, not before taking precautions. The huge wooden-bladed wheel must have been about thirty meters high and was held in the air by a central axle, connected to a stone wall. I was afraid to get too close, since it seemed ancient and might collapse. It was a construction that didn't look like anything I had seen so far. Its size, its shape, were unknown to me.

"I hate heights! What trouble do I always get into because of you. Of course, don't say anything, you start climbing the wheel and leave me on the ground. How many days have we been together, three, four? Well who cares, I don't know why I bother talking to you..."

We heard the sermon a man was giving the other, while the two of them climbed the huge crown.

"Heyyy! What are you doing up there?" I shouted, and the man stopped talking to the other; he looked at us and said:

"Climbing, climbing, don't stay down there, it's dangerous down there."

My worst fears were confirmed when I heard a noise coming downstream. We climbed the huge blades, but when we reached the height of a fourth floor the water came filling the dry streambed and crashing against the structures. It took a long time for them to start moving, as they must have weighed tons. It slowly accelerated and began lifting us up; when we reached the height of the central axle, the two men gave us a hand to climb onto the stone construction holding it.

"I'm Alb, and you are?"

"They call me Bear and I think he's called Pasca; he's a little slow and doesn't talk much..."

Inside that construction a bunch of thick leather belts drove some pulleys and rubbed against a metal sphere charging it with static electricity. Small lightning bolts began jumping from the top which grew in size when the contraption accelerated. Everything lit up; we were enveloped in a kind of whitish mist, so bright it blinded us for a few moments. The energy from the primitive generator made us jump to another bubble.

THEY ALL WALKED TOGETHER in a line down the long eastward hallway. They passed the entrances to many dwellings, some with the door ajar, as if someone was watching them through the peephole from the other side. Their breath condensed into a cloud when they exhaled. The walls shone as if covered with millions of tiny crystal fragments. They reached the end of the first hallway, lit only by the guard's flashlight. He tapped the wall with his closed hand, listening carefully to the sound it made, in order to get an idea of the thickness.

"It's not a very thick wall, with some tools we can drill through it easily."

Even though it wasn't very solid, at least a heavy object would be needed to hit the wall like a hammer.

"There's an open door here, we can probably find something useful on this floor," Barbara communicated to the rest of the group, standing right in front of the entrance. Everyone turned to look at her, but no one said anything. She pushed the door, freezing cold to the touch, and it moved with a shriek that made their hair stand on end. A small entrance hall could be seen, and farther ahead a door with a window at its center through which a faint light streamed. She tried to take the first step, but her legs shook with fear. In a fraction of a second, thousands of terrifying scenes flashed through her mind. The whole group was starting to suspect that something strange was happening and it wasn't just the weather that concerned them. In any case, they didn't need a prodigious imagination to envision the scenes that must have occurred in many of the houses. The extreme cold and the sepulchral silence enveloping everything foretold that there had to be piles of corpses everywhere. Surely people had died of hypothermia, curled up and huddled in their beds or sitting on their sofas.

"Silence, quiet! I think I heard a voice," she whispered, sticking her head inside that eerie place. She was practically paralyzed by fear and felt her bladder contract with electric spasms, causing incontinence.

"Did you hear it? A woman's voice."

As soon as she said this, she ran back out into the hallway again. The rest of the group also heard something. But although they all seemed to be acting brave, they looked at each other and no one dared to enter.

"Let me through, I'll go," Kira told them calmly.

She was used to seeing all kinds of unpleasant images, just one day in the emergency room left you immune to fright. She walked through the darkness, straight toward the dim light at the back. The moment she put her hand on the handle, shouts and screams came from behind her. Her heart beat faster and she had to hurry out to see what was happening. She found Tim lying on the floor, with streaks of blood gushing from his head. The prisoner who had been at the back of the group until then, leaning against the wall with his hands taped behind his back, didn't know what was going on. Seeing everyone was distracted, he thought it was a good time to escape. He came charging at the team, head first, like a bull. They had to jump out of the way quickly to avoid being mowed down by that raging locomotive. But as I mentioned, he didn't know what was happening and ran straight into the wall they were trying to tear down. He rammed his huge skull against it and managed to get his melon through to the other side. Then he collapsed. Clearly this man's head wasn't functioning properly, but with the blow he'd received, his brain might actually fall back into place and he'd regain his common sense.

While they stared at the bull lying on the floor moaning from the tremendous crash, they heard the voice coming from the apartment again, this time all the team members heard it clearly. Again the doctor set off, this time without hesitation. She reached the back and opened the door. She held her breath for a second before looking at that

Dante-esque scene, but let it out immediately when she saw the room was uninhabited. The light and voice were coming from a small television on the living room table. It was one of those portable sets powered by batteries. The broadcast only showed bands of color, like an old test pattern. The same announcement they had heard on the radio kept playing on loop. On the table there was a glass of milk and a plate of cookies. The chair was positioned as if someone had been eating while watching TV. As she studied the scene to try to draw some conclusion about what had happened, out of the corner of her eye she saw something move in the shadows in one corner of the room.

"Is someone there?" she asked in a quivering voice, but no one answered. She focused on that area and again saw something move, it was a silhouette, a dark shape about six feet tall. She steeled herself and moved closer. A gust of cold air hit her in the face. A window let in a draft that intermittently moved a curtain. Her subconscious had conjured up the silhouette of a person. Only that fabric seemed to have life in that place. On her way back she told the group what had transpired and they all went in inspecting every millimeter of the residence. After finding everything as if the inhabitants had disappeared due to spontaneous combustion, speculation began:

"This has me very puzzled..." said Phill.

As always, direct and brief.

Now it was Mr. Chang's turn; but since none of the attendees understood a single word he was articulating with great effort, accompanied by profuse gesturing with his hands and even making faces, and because none of us could make out the bunch of noises, I won't transcribe them, as I'm not even sure a Chinese person would be able to understand.

Then the policeman spoke up. You're probably wondering why up to now I haven't told you his name. Simply put, no one in the group had asked him, and neither had I...

"I think," said the guard, "a leak at the nuclear plant caused all this mess. I'm sure the radiation was able to disintegrate bodies, making the corpses disappear. I don't remember in which country of the former Soviet Union it happened, but I distinctly remember the cadavers had vaporized. What was the name of that magazine? My...Millennium, Millenia, Millennialism, well, doesn't matter. I know it was one of those science journals."

"Ha! He says science journals. Those magazines are full of tall tales," the bank director scoffed mockingly.

"You shouldn't laugh, Steve; you know very well what's happening here is out of the ordinary. I may not have an education and have only gotten as far as driving an armored vehicle, but tell me how you explain what's going on."

A profound silence ensued and they looked at the little panic-prone man, who had had his hand up for a while, asking for a turn to speak as if he were in school.

"He's right," said Barbara, "just because you don't believe in certain things doesn't mean they don't happen. We're used to seeing even more far-fetched stories become reality on the news. It's not as if I decided to ignore Samuel's turn, disregarding him, it's just what happened: they left him with his hand up without letting him get a word out."

"Most likely," Kira added, "the emergency plan went into effect and the government ordered the population evacuated to the safest locations. Surely they took everyone to the school, where they would have equipment, provisions, heating, medical attention..."

"That, that's exactly what I'm trying to say; I'm sure they evacuated everyone because some kind of virus has contaminated the city. Maybe genetically modified foods... I'm certain this is a pandemic. A viral epidemic that has infected the entire population. We're definitely already infected from entering this house and touching everything... There's no escaping this, we're going to die, I need to disinfect my hands: where's the bathroom? I have to wash up right away. I knew it, we won't survive..."

Samuel continued to frantically look for the bathroom. He pushed open the door and rushed in, yelling incessantly and continuing his anxious monologue. Bad luck would have it that when he stepped on the entry mat, it got tangled around his feet and he fell face first into the bathtub.

"Dear God, dear God, I'm going to die! But what am I saying, I'm an atheist... Aaah! This is full of remains, blood, corpses everywhere... no, no, someone's grabbing me..."

The guard shone his flashlight towards the area where Samuel was splashing around as if drowning. He had some socks on his head and was wrestling hand-to-hand with a pair of overalls as if it were a man. It seems someone had put this type of clothing in the tub to wash.

"I'm suffocating, I can't breathe, I have the virus all over my body, I'm completely contaminated."

"Can someone hand me a bag?" Kira asked resignedly.

It hadn't been long since the great floods in which many people lost everything they owned, but the material losses weren't the most important thing. In that terrible environmental catastrophe, millions of people disappeared around the world. Now the weather was lashing out against people again with this ice storm. You didn't have to be a scholar to realize something was happening, that the Earth was responding to the lifestyle humans had chosen. The majority opted for a consumerist way of life, the culture of capitalism, trying to acquire everything that can be purchased. They neglected gratitude towards the provider, towards Mother Earth. They wanted to detach themselves from her, differentiating and distancing themselves from anything natural. They felt safer in their buildings made of cold, inert metal and concrete.

Kira had a good friend who spent over fifteen years of his life researching the production of non-polluting biofuels from bacterial cultures fed with organic waste, with trash. By providing nourishment to microorganisms and having them recycle our waste, biofuels, bioplastics and even a cheap protein source that could be used as food were generated in a symbiotic relationship with nature. And what did he gain after all those years of work? Criticism, insults, and despair. The power structure built on possessions cannot allow everyone to have free access to energy and food. There's a saying in my country that goes: "If shit had value, the poor would be born without assholes."

I remember when I was little, my house seemed huge to me, and my small town appeared gigantic, my country was like infinite. As I grew up, my house started feeling smaller, my town seemed to shrink, and I traveled across my country by bicycle. Today I chat with my friends in Japan, America, or anywhere else in the world and I can see on my computer how small our planet is. What's wrong with those people who deny that humans have the capacity to alter the Earth's climate? They think resources are inexhaustible, that trees can be cut down recklessly because forests and jungles are infinite, that overfishing doesn't deplete the oceans, that whales will never become extinct, that they live in an infinite world... I think they haven't mentally matured past the age of four. Maybe they just need time, perhaps if they lived two hundred or three hundred years they would realize the mistakes they've made.

They couldn't spend too much time debating the issue and had to continue on their way. The wall was easy to get through once Tim opened it up with his head. They used some tools they found in the house and made an opening with ease. On the other side, a new dark hallway; the guard shined his flashlight, but the bulb started blinking, indicating the batteries were about to run out.

"I, I, I, I have some candles and matches! Although they won't be any use, because we're all contaminated..."

"Give them here!"

And Phil took the candles and matches out of Samuel's hands, to try to light them.

"It seems that in addition to being a hypochondriac, he has some other problem, like the habit of taking and keeping in his pockets everything he finds along the way."

There was no way those matches would light; they were completely soaked. No one had a lighter; they were about to be left in the dark; that way it would be impossible for them to move in the right direction, and what was even worse, the building seemed like a real labyrinth, without light they wouldn't be able to find their way back to look for another exit. But before panic could set in, the resourceful policeman put his brilliant mind in motion and dismantled the flashlight, broke the glass bulb and put it back in place, then positioned the candle wick in contact with it.

"I hope this works," he commented before pressing the flashlight switch. The glowing filament began catching the wick and with a gentle puff the flame appeared. He waited a few seconds for the wax to start melting; then lit the others with it. On the move again, this time lit by candles and walking single file; they looked like members of a procession.

Tiredness and cold were taking their toll on their strength. Having lost track of time in that maze of hallways, they decided they had to stop and rest, but in that spot there were no doors, only long, narrow corridors with vaulted ceilings, constructed as a single piece like concrete tunnels. In their breakthroughs knocking down walls, they must have entered some old service passages, the kind used in the war as shelters during aerial bombardmcnts.

"Did you hear that?"

But Phil hadn't heard anything. The policeman kept walking slowly, a candle in his hand forming a yellowish halo around him. The circle of light was very small and beyond a few meters only silhouettes could be made out in the shadows. He'd had the feeling for a while that someone was watching him, maybe his imagination was starting to play tricks on him due to extreme exhaustion. Several times he thought he saw the shape of a man at the end of the hallway, but he would rub his tired eyes and when he looked again to see better he didn't find anything there. He could hear footsteps keeping pace with his, to camouflage them with his own.

"Look, over there! Did you see it?"

"But what was that?"

"You saw it too?"

"Yes, of course, a man was crouching up ahead and then he ran off."

"I've been hearing and seeing him for a while, but I thought it was just fatigue influencing my subconscious."

The group stopped short; the passage was so narrow they could only go single file. In this arrangement it was very difficult to talk to the whole group. As the policeman turned to tell the rest of the team to back up to a wider area, he heard hurried footsteps approaching, as if someone was taking giant strides toward him. He started pushing the others in a panic, yelling for them to back up, to run. Their voices made everyone move back, but he remained at the rear, pushing the group as best he could. He could hear asthmatic breathing, long and pronounced. Nervous, he kept lighting up behind him trying to keep the candle from going out; he couldn't see anything; Chinese shadows everywhere seemed to be lurking around him. They finally managed to reach a wider section where the tunnel opened up into a small chamber.

"There's something lurking in the dark!"

"Come on! If Samuel's saying it..." but for a policeman to be so scared of some shadows.

"No shadows, I know perfectly well what I saw and heard."

"Rats, they were probably just rats."

I saw something too...

"How is this possible: the bigger the guys nowadays, the bigger cowards they are..." the bank director remarked angrily, a short man who was rubbing his bald head with his chubby hands as he spoke.

"I'm absolutely certain I saw something, and when I say something I don't mean just anything. I saw a human figure, I could see his face and his black eyes and he's not a man, whatever he is, it's not of this world."

"Remembering the explanation you gave a few hours ago about the nuclear plant and the disappearance of the people, I think you have a very creative mind. Well, seeing as everyone agrees with my theory, it would be best to get moving again."

"No one's getting me back in that place..."

"Enough already, I'm tired of cowards, I'll go first ladies," he said, visibly annoyed, red-faced, and rubbing his head from forehead to nape.

The gallery must have been several meters underground, because the temperature there was stable. On the other hand, it was very strange they hadn't encountered any living things, but no one seemed to notice. They didn't even see cockroaches.

I'VE BEEN THINKING for a few days about what happened. Was time unalterable? Was the future already written and couldn't be changed? It was still too early to make any affirmation. The other day's incident in the kitchen may have been a mere coincidence. There were still many days left and it wasn't good to jump to conclusions.

PEOPLE HAVE VERY DIFFERENT qualities: there are people who can play an instrument well, piano, violin; individuals who can paint and draw portraits with impressive skill. There are those who are good at math, with a prodigious memory capable of storing endless amounts of data. Well, these people tend to be considered geniuses because they stand out in some unconventional activity. If we look more closely at most of these gifted people, we'll realize they invest many hours in whatever they're good at. They train constantly, so much so they normally neglect other tasks. But why does no one reward common qualities? We all have more or less the same lifespan, and therefore the same time to practice; some devote it to playing the trumpet and others, like my neighbors, dedicate it to chatting and gossiping about events happening in the neighborhood. Then there are undervalued trades, no one appreciates the genius who has been practicing laying bricks for over 30 years. I know many famous musicians, actors, painters, etc. for their work, but I don't know a single bricklayer, carpenter, "maybe the family of the Nazarene who had to climb a mountain and start yelling," much less a greengrocer, fishmonger... But these people invest many hours in their work, the gossiping neighbors don't stop for an instant in the practice of gossiping. They must have some skill. "Maybe if they were hired by the FBI. My neighbor can interrogate you in under two minutes. The time it takes for the elevator to go down the nine floors." Many of the other geniuses, the famous ones, don't even know how to tie their shoelaces and are incapable of holding a conversation; they have devoted all their time to practicing only their one skill and have neglected everything else.

I remember a rather bad joke, where three volunteers are sent into space, each from a different country and each with a single object in the rocket. The German takes musical instruments, the whole ship full of pianos, violins, trumpets... The Frenchman asks to be accompanied by women. The Spaniard demands the transport be filled with tobacco: "Pipe tobacco, cigarettes and cigars of every brand..." The rockets take off and the days pass slowly. After ten years the ships prepare to return to Earth. The German's arrives first, the doors open and a man comes out playing the violin marvelously; the melody is so fantastic that everyone cries with emotion. The crowd goes wild, everyone wants to see and touch the genius. Then the Frenchman's vessel arrives. People crowd around to see this man. The doors open and countless children come out of the rocket. Everyone congratulates the man: he's extraordinary. Finally the Spaniard's rocket touches ground and the doors open. The crowd awaits feverishly for the new genius to emerge. A disheveled man comes out of the spacecraft, looking like a castaway, running through the crowd and shouting: a lighter, please, a lighter...

"I've always wondered: What would the Spaniard do for those 10 years? He must have spent his time on something! Maybe he's a virtuoso of meditation and philosophy..."

THE FEELING AFTER MOVING from one bubble to another was already bad enough, but also, in this one the smell was unbearable. The water reached up to our waists, it was tepid and fermenting. That swamp was like a sort of breeding ground. Foul gases were continually emanating that were hundreds of times more putrid than a pigsty. The water was rotting and bubbles constantly burst on the surface, ceaselessly adding more nauseating vapors. It was difficult to walk through that marshland. The soft, hot, muddy bottom was like a living being; it grabbed our feet like hands.

We moved toward some trees that could be seen rising on the horizon. To avoid getting stuck to the ground and falling when losing our balance, we decided to walk side by side. All together, shoulder to shoulder, like a group of drunks dancing at a wedding.

Finally, we managed to reach the small island. A few tall, slender trees with cauliflower-shaped tops, possibly acacias, which must have been over ninety feet tall, were what could be seen at first glance. Farther in, a surface of stones could be seen. They were river rocks rounded by erosion, the size of a fist and white in color. They were as smooth as talc.

A river divided the island. A dam formed by black boulders the size of coconuts created a small reservoir.

The Bear approached the lagoon:

"Come, come, look what's at the bottom!"

We all rushed over quickly, spurred by curiosity.

At the bottom of the lake, a huge construction could be clearly seen through its crystalline waters. A colossus of white marble, with legs apart, bridged the gap between the two pink stone walls. It was hard to estimate its height since it was under water. But based on proportions it could easily reach 150 feet.

"Listen, I think I know what we have to do to get out of this bubble," said the Bear. His plan was to remove some of the stones that formed the dam, allowing the water to drain out and leaving the reservoir empty. Then we could walk down the gently sloping banks to the bottom. Once there, we would enter through the arch formed by the giant statue's legs.

Since the plan was simple and seemingly flawless, we all got to work. We formed a chain: one person removed stones and passed them to the others.

After working for about an hour or so and seeing how much was left, the Bear started singing old military songs to lift our spirits. Before we knew it, we were all singing.

On the other side, the dry riverbed formed by white stones reminded me of that place I had descended with Alb, where we met The Bear and Pasca. Of course, that was it; everything was connected in some way.

"I don't think you should keep removing stones, stop for a moment."

But it was already too late; the weakened walls of the dam started collapsing and the water flowed forcefully flooding the riverbed. The reservoir emptied and in the center of the muddy bottom was the distortion that would transport us to the next sphere.

TIME PASSES QUICKLY, fleetingly, leaving flashes of small memories when one is happy. I've often burned entire albums, permanently destroying those photographic memories. I wish I could do the same with my memories. The truth is good memories only cause me pain, longing for times past. Better times that will never return, reminding me of the ephemeral nature of this existence. Over time, bad ones don't seem so bad, and you can even be glad to remember them, because you feel good about having left them behind. Maybe we should only remember the difficult moments. Perhaps we should only photograph ourselves during sad times. That kind of image could surely lift our spirits. But instead, we always take pictures at the best times, on vacations, holidays, creating idyllic images of a past time that stab the soul with their memory. I often wonder who those characters are, those people who appear in my photos. Is it me? Are they my friends? Where are they now? Where did those sunny days go? Beach days, river days, green, bright, full of hope. Time destroyed all that, friends left, summer ended, the party finished and the songs lost their meaning.

Happy Times

I WONDER: WHAT IS HAPPINESS? Time constantly redefines the answer. Now I would choose any boring day from my childhood summer vacations as perfect times. The days were long, almost endless. The sun seemed to always shine high above. Dazzling memories, in vivid colors. The clock without hands showed an infinite future.

KIRA MANAGED TO CONVINCE the guard to position himself second to last, so he would be one of those carrying the injured man. They went back into those gloomy ducts, advancing in the candlelight. Steve walked with a firm step, with the typical bravery of heroes or fools. Some sections seemed to be covered in something soft, which could be felt when stepping on it, like walking on grapes. But no one paid too much attention to this event and they continued on their way. The silence was interrupted by gunshots, they could see the cavern lighting up in the distance with fleeting glimmers.

"Help, help!" a man's voice was heard and they all quickened their pace. They arrived at the door of a room and the banker went in without thinking twice. As soon as he poked his head in, he found two men lying on the floor; both dressed as police, one face down and the other half sitting up, holding his leg as if it were fractured. The other one, whose face couldn't be seen, looked as if his skin had been burned, as if boiling oil or some kind of acid had been poured on him. The scene was strange and shocking. The corpse had a gun close by, still stuck to one hand, and a thin trail of smoke could be seen rising from the barrel. The other man, on the other hand, had no weapon and seemed perfectly fine, only holding his leg as if he had been struck. Something didn't seem to add up in that scenario. The rest of the group members remained outside, waiting to be told if the place was safe. The guard also entered the room and surveyed the scene. He remained pensive for a few seconds. The policeman, sitting on the floor, extended his hand asking for help getting up. The banker approached to lend him a hand.

"No! Come back here!" the guard yelled nervously, but the banker looked at him bewildered, making a contemptuous face, as if a madman was speaking to him. While he stood with his back turned, looking at the guard with that mocking expression, the policeman still on the floor stared straight at his face, with those evil dark eyes he had seen earlier in the dark. He smiled broadly, stretching his mouth wider and wider, reaching from ear to ear. His long, sharp teeth looked like a shark's. The guard was paralyzed with fear. The banker, who still held his stupid grimace, turned holding out his hand to the injured man and, at that very instant, looked the monster right in the face. A moment of surprise, then that being ripped off his arm with one bite. The pain showed on his face. The creature transformed into a dark mass and completely engulfed the man who wasn't even able to scream due to his state of shock. The guard quickly left that room, slamming the door shut violently. He leaned against it and slid down until landing on his bottom on the floor. Paralyzed by terror he was unable to process what had happened. The door started shaking as if an enormous force was pushing it from the inside. He held the handle tightly and with effort managed to block it, handcuffing it. Then he collapsed again, sitting with his back against the entrance.

"Mooo! Moo! Mooo!"

That was the noise Tim made through his nostrils, since his mouth was sealed by the gag. Everyone remained silent. Samuel approached and removed the tape, allowing him to speak.

"Crazy, murderer! That cop is crazy, he killed Mr. Steve..."

They were all dumbfounded.

"You, you're the crazy one! I haven't killed anyone, I don't know how to explain what happened in there. What was stalking us in the dark swallowed Steve."

"Who believes that story? What happened is you locked him in there because he was the only one in the group who stood up to you."

"Help, let me out!"

They heard the banker's pleading voice.

"And now what? How are you going to continue this charade?"

Barbara approached the door to open it and free Mr. Steve.

"No, no, wait, that thing in there isn't Steve!"

"No, no, no! Bad, very bad a "devil" — said old man Chang. Although perplexed, the woman accepted the policeman's words, as they seemed completely sincere to her. She then spoke in a low voice with the group, while the thing inside continued begging them to open the door. She asked them for a vote of confidence and they agreed to do the following test: he and the other employees knew the bank director was gay. So Barbara asked him:

"Honey, are you okay? The girl and I are worried."

"Yes my love, I just bumped my head, open up so we can go home."

"You see that's not Steve, I don't know what that thing is, but it's certainly not human," he whispered to the rest of the group, but as he did so, that being started banging on the door so hard that the wood began splintering. Then they all ran off; not even Tim wanted to stay and see what was shaking the door so violently.

After running through that huge underground complex for who knows how long, stimulated by the adrenaline rush, they managed to reach some stairs that went up. An ornate iron door blocked their way, but as always, the guard managed to open it easily. They all immediately recognized that place: they were in the library, right across from the school. The dim light coming through the windows allowed them to see without artificial light. They were very tired and once they felt safe, exhaustion hit them like a slab. In the hallway they found a vending machine with chocolate bars, also a water dispenser, one of those with a huge tank on top and plastic conical cups to use as glasses. They quickly stocked up and although their bodies didn't respond, having their goal so close encouraged them to continue.

"We should stay here; if we haven't been infected yet it's best we remain isolated from others. The meeting point will be full of dying people and the only thing we can do there is get infected. I'm certain that if we go we'll die."

Samuel began one of his endless monologues, accelerating as usual, finally reaching a panic attack, as was common for the rest of the individuals, not only unaffected by it, but reassured that everything had returned to normal. No one wanted to talk about what had happened below ground, maybe it wasn't the right time, or perhaps it was better to forget it, like a nightmare, a bad dream. The memories were so vague, so confusing, the darkness, the tiredness...

No one was obligated to remain in the community; circumstances brought this disparate group of people together to face the disaster and united they had a better chance of survival. The group unanimously decided it was best to get to the emergency meeting place as soon as possible. The sick man couldn't wait any longer, he had to be treated immediately.

Phil looked out one of the windows and then, to everyone's surprise, opened it slightly. A gust of wind came in, but with barely a tenth of the force they were all expecting. It seemed the storm was letting up, perhaps it would subside temporarily. It was the ideal time to cross the street. They set off leaving Samuel behind, who continued with his particular lecture. Finding himself alone, he heard a noise, looked from side to side, the shelves were full of books and some tables had a few open on them, as if the people who had been reading them had disappeared spontaneously. The hairs on his neck stood up and he began talking to himself. He dashed out like lightning and caught up with the group exiting through the main entrance. They crossed the avenue holding on to each other, managing this way to stay on their feet, as the ground was very slippery. As they drew near, they could see lights inside the classrooms, the emergency generators set up for these cases seemed to be working. They climbed the white marble steps giving access to the interior; behind the thick wooden doors was a plastic foyer, tarps set up like a modular tent; they blocked entry into the premises with an airtight zipper. Kira was very familiar with this kind of system, they were the typical measures taken in case of biological hazard. This time it wasn't Samuel who addressed the group with his typical apocalyptic words, in this case it was her:

"Cover your faces with rags or with your sweater collars and avoid touching anything. The school is sealed to prevent biological contamination, it's a standard procedure used as a preventive measure."

Having said this, she took the lead of the group and opened the plastic entrance, unsealing it. The lights emitted a very white glare and after their eyes had become accustomed to the dark, it took them a while to adjust. The generator was repeatedly failing, lowering the intensity of the lighting intermittently. They went down the central hallway; the classrooms were closed. As they walked they opened the doors of the rooms on either side, but everything was deserted. They started yelling but no one answered, the school seemed completely empty.

"Calm down, stay calm, we'll keep going to the gym, for sure everyone's gathered there."

They walked down the wide orange brick corridor lined with elementary school children's drawings. The scene was quite surrealistic, they seemed like shipwreck survivors walking through those pristine, sterile hallways, as if the storm had never happened.

The entrance to the sports area was once again sealed with a transparent vinyl foyer and corresponding airtight zipper. The doctor opened the door and they entered what were the basketball courts. The room put their nerves on edge. The entire enclosure was fitted out with white hospital beds, placed a hair's breadth away from each other. From the ceiling, a cable descended to each of them, entering through the top portion of the plastic cover placed over the cots like a mosquito net. The cables powered a lamp focused right on the center of each mattress. They were biological containment units, which allowed treating patients without risk of contagion. They walked among the containment units, hoping to see someone, but they didn't find absolutely anything. The room was huge and hundreds, perhaps thousands of prepared beds were empty. The generator, failing more and more frequently, left them in darkness for a few seconds and then restarted with difficulty squeezing out the last drops of gasoline. When they were more or less halfway, the fuel finally ran out completely and they were left in the dark. They didn't know if they would find people in the beds at the back, the semi-transparent plastic covering them didn't allow clearly seeing the interior. Samuel began breathing nervously, as if he wasn't getting enough air into his lungs; he was so terrified he didn't dare say a word. He thought that if there was something out there in the dark and he spoke, it would discover his location and pounce on him. Afterwards, after remaining paralyzed for a few instants, they slowly started walking. The sound of footsteps produced a prolonged echo. No one said anything, only their footsteps and choppy breathing could be heard. One of the beds in the back rolled forward on its wheels, then objects made of glass began falling, noisily shattering on the floor, and a figure ran across the room. Something bulky, anthropomorphic in shape, exited through the emergency door.

"Hey!"

"Shhh, don't reveal our location!" Samuel interrupted, but Kira insisted:

"Hey! Are you in charge?"

Her words reverberated, bouncing off the walls of the room. There was no answer. Samuel, nervous, wanted to escape that chilling place and ran for the emergency exit, clearly visible due to its fluorescent signage. He placed both hands on the bar that activated the opening mechanism, but an opposing force pushed him back. The door opened and an enormous being with a gigantic head entered. Samuel slipped falling on his back to the floor and tried to move away from that thing, but the slick floor made him slide and he couldn't get anywhere. Then the monster pounced on him. The man let out a shriek that left them deaf. The being also shrieked drawing back, turned on a flashlight and shone it directly in Samuel's face, who wouldn't stop screaming. It was a man wearing an NBC suit (a suit that protects the user from contaminating chemical, biological or radioactive agents).

"What a joy to see you!" he exclaimed with poor enunciation and unzipped the suit, poking his head out. He was a man with a very round, large head, and a face redder than a tomato.

"Meee name León, yes that's my name."

Without finishing his sentence he grabbed a canteen hanging from a belt around his waist and took a good swig.

"Anís Sanblas, the old faithful, the best in the whole world."

The man was totally plastered, barely able to stand.

THE DAYS ARE SLOWLY running out, escaping through my fingers like water. Again and again I've tried altering events but even changing some things, the results have been exactly the same. There seems to be a script written in some way; it's as if every tiny bit of matter has a number, a code like products at the supermarket, and knows exactly where it belongs.

"I didn't travel through time just to watch her die again without being able to do anything!"

THE ENTRANCE, AS ALWAYS, left you a bit confused, you needed some time to process what had happened. The flash of light made you lose consciousness for a few seconds. Then I noticed that strong smell of damp earth. The ground was reddish sand and seemed to have been freshly rained on. We were in the middle of a crossroads, the main road bordered by a row of small trees, in perfect formation. Downward, the main road disappeared on the horizon. To the right and left the other smaller road, which looked more like a path marked in the sand, ended as far as the eye could see, on one side and the other, surely marking the limits of the bubble. I then turned around. A gust of wind hit my face and I was amazed at the imposing view. My eyes followed the road uphill into the distance and then focused on a huge building, orange-yellow in color, made of baked and polished clay. First, an enormous rectangle rested at the foot of the road; even from a distance, its size covered the entire horizon. My eyes followed the walls of that colossal structure upward and I felt myself shrinking, becoming very small, like an ant at the feet of a titan. The building ascended in a pyramid shape, rectangle on top of rectangle reaching as far as the eye could see. The sun was eclipsed, with some of its rays peeking out from the sides of the enormous building. I looked at my companions, motionless with astonished faces before that gigantic edifice. I turned my eyes again to such a colossal image and was once more amazed by its grandeur.

"Alb, where could this have come from?"

"Let's go, let's go!"

I immediately realized everyone had started toward the building; the professor glanced back for an instant to say these words. I could see a look of childlike happiness on his face. I started running a bit to catch up with them.

"It must be the work of an ancient civilization; perhaps it's a piece of space-time trapped in the bubble belonging to Atlantis. But let's not waste time and get closer to see it in more detail."

Alb was really enjoying it like a kid.

Although The Bear and Pasca were also not wasting any time. For no reason at all, the expedition seemed to have turned into an athletics competition. We all wanted to get there first. The race soon became a kind of marathon, since the enormous foundation deceived the senses, appearing to be very near, when in reality there was a good distance to reach its base. Finally, sweaty and tired we all arrived at the foot of the tower. I didn't notice which of us was first or last to get there, since it took me a while to catch my breath. As we breathed heavily, trying to breathe normally again, we looked at each other and smiled, making stupid happy faces. Right away I saw Alb running his hands over the smooth mud wall, brushing off the clumped dust and uncovering some markings that looked like symbols from some ancient language.

"They follow a pattern! They form a cycle! Wait, wait, I've got it: they're prime numbers. The text is written so that anyone using the universal language of mathematics can decipher it."

The professor was undoubtedly the most active and lively person on the team, despite his age. His eyes lit up as he contemplated those symbols, with the same gleam as a child's gaze when receiving Christmas gifts.

He made mental calculations while mumbling some words and taking notes by making tracings with a finger in the sand at his feet. The Bear observed him trying to understand some of the words he was muttering and Pasca... Where was Pasca? Where had he gone? I looked from side to side along the walls of the structure in the distance, but I didn't spot him anywhere. I looked back at the group and saw our footprints on the ground. Mine, The Bear's, Alb's and also Pasca's, which left no doubt, since you could clearly see the prints left by one of his shoes missing a piece of sole. I followed his steps several meters along the edge of the immense wall and then, they simply vanished. It seemed Pasca had been swallowed by the earth itself. I felt a lump in my throat and my heart skipped a beat, thinking he might have been swallowed by the wormoids, but I found it strange not to hear anything, and even more so, not detecting their foul smell. I examined the area more closely, focusing on the shiny, smooth mud wall, soft as the clay surface of an earthenware jug. Then I noticed something abnormal, the diaphanous surface seemed to have a peculiarity, an odd brightness right where Pasca's footprints ended. I then looked up and there atop, four or five stories high, was Pasca, looking like an insect clinging to the base of a skyscraper.

"Heyyyy!" he yelled, waving a hand somewhat awkwardly to greet us. I thought he would fall and crack his skull on the ground at any moment. But he seemed quite comfortable. The unusual shape of the structure appeared to conceal a sort of chute that ascended as far as the eye could see like a chimney attached to the wall.

"Exactly! That's it, that's what the message means: He who has the courage to climb to the sky, will find the open gates of the great temple."

And in less time than it took me to blink, Alb was climbing the tower, following Pasca's footsteps. Then The Bear followed him. I had no intention of embarking on this absurd adventure. I had a lot of practice climbing mountains when I was into mountaineering as a young man and I knew very well that the beginning always seems easy, but very often halfway up you regret having climbed at all. It's not at all pleasant to find yourself several hundred meters up and not have the strength to either keep climbing or get back down.

The wind whistled pushing me and messing up my hair; then silence filled everything and I don't know if it was my imagination but I started smelling that disgusting aroma again. I jumped up and clambered onto the wall, starting to ascend using an old climbing technique. With a position similar to crawling but vertically instead of horizontally, with my back pressing against one of the walls and hands and feet on the other, I climbed up easily catching up to the rest of the group. The truth is it seemed quite simple, the only thing was that since it formed a "U" and not a closed chimney, the view became more and more impressive as we gained altitude. It was clear none of us in the group suffered from vertigo.

The temperature dropped as the expedition continued ascending. Although at ground level the weather had been almost summery, now my hands were starting to get cold. The race to catch up with the group had dampened my clothes with sweat and the wind, which was blowing stronger and stronger, chilled my chest which was still wet. My teeth chattered, but I clenched my jaw tightly to silence them. The crevice in the wall narrowed as we advanced. My back barely fit anymore, almost half of me was outside the wall and the wind shook my clothes, waving them like a flag.

I didn't intend at this point to reminisce about my early climbing days without ropes, armed with stupidity and ignorance. Above all I didn't want to remember how sometimes lessons are learned the hard way, having a really bad time and regretting being stupid enough to get myself into that predicament. Often experience can be a negative factor, because the worst thing halfway up a ropeless climb is self-doubt. Ignorance can give you false courage, since you're not really aware of how easily you can make a mistake and fall into the abyss. With my back increasingly farther out, I started telling myself it had been a mistake to climb the wall. Nerves were starting to take hold of me and this was the worst thing that could happen, because in this state you waste a lot of energy and my limbs soon started to feel heavy. My arms were asleep and I was seeing I would fall any minute.

"Come on! We're here!" said Alb from the top of the first rectangle forming the colossal structure.

"Come on, a little more...!" he continued, holding out a hand to me lying on his chest from the ledge. I finally breathed relieved and jumped grabbing onto the terrace ledge with both hands. But my numb limbs failed me and I slipped. That's right, that's how tragedies often happen, when you let your guard down; it's at the silliest moment that you fall and kill yourself. There was nothing left to do. I didn't feel scared, instead I felt ashamed to die in such an absurd way. I felt my body become weightless as I accelerated toward the ground in the fall. The professor's bright, alive eyes quickly moved away from me.

"I've got you!"

And I felt his hand grab me firmly by the arm. With effort I braced my legs against the smooth orange ceramic of the wall and managed to climb onto the balcony.

"What a fright!" I told Alb euphorically due to the adrenaline rush. He looked at me smiling as if nothing had happened.

The rest of the team was sitting, resting on the very spacious terrace. When I recovered from the scare, I could enjoy the magnificent views. We seemed to be in the sky, the clouds passed close by, looking as if they were made of cotton; when they were nearer, they enveloped us in their misty interior.

The sun was starting to set; it seemed in this bubble there were cycles of night and day, but from my observations they were accelerated, since we couldn't have been here more than seven or eight hours and when we entered the sun was high marking an early morning hour.

"Yes, I noticed it too," commented the old man.

Apparently I had been thinking out loud.

"By my calculations a full cycle must be completed every 12 hours," he continued explaining. Which gives us about five hours to rest. I don't think those disgusting devil worms are capable of climbing the walls."

Pasca put his hands in his pockets and started leaving piles of berries in mounds.

"You can eat them without worry, I tried them many hours ago and they're edible," said the man softly offering us those wild fruits.

He didn't talk much and something about his way of expressing himself and his appearance gave the impression that he was mentally impaired, but the truth is he was demonstrating to us that he didn't have a foolish bone in his body.

The greens contained a large amount of fructose, which helped us recover from the exertion. Also, I had gone a long time without eating; here it was hard to calculate time but I guess at least a couple of days.

We rested for a while and soon the sun appeared on the horizon again.

"Let's go boys, it's time to continue!"

I looked at the professor and there he was, standing ready to keep going without any signs of tiredness. The rest of the team remained curled up on the ground, looking sleepy. He held out his hand and helped me get up.

"Let's go son, it's a splendid day for climbing!"

I looked at the summit, and the building seemed endless, with clouds covering the highest part. We climbed without paying attention to the altitude, we had been clinging to the stone surface for so long that the height no longer impressed us. We were so high up that the ground could not be seen, the clouds enveloped us as we ascended and although it took us a bit to get going after the rest, once we warmed up we felt invigorated again. Finally, I heard Pasca's voice, who was leading the group, somewhat ahead given his skill for climbing:

"We're here! We made it!"

I climbed the last stretch dragging myself, and when I poked my head out I saw the top, a flat surface with a huge granite portico in the center. Carved into its enormous pillars were multitudes of symbols that Alb immediately began deciphering. The rest of us were sitting resting on the ground.

"Of course, the symbols have to be arranged in order! But where are they? We have to find some sort of actuators with carved lunar cycles!"

We started scouring the entire structure looking for those symbols, but we didn't find anything. I hope we don't have to climb back down to look for the damned buttons at the base of the pyramid. We were absorbed, completely devoted to our task and didn't realize Pasca hadn't gotten up and had had his hand raised the whole time. When we paused pensively looking at him, he put his hand down and pointed to the tile he was sitting on.

"It's not possible; the engravings are under our feet and we didn't even notice! I don't know what we'd do without this boy..."

According to the professor, we had to activate the system by pressing the tiles following the correct combination. We each stood in front of one of them, waiting for the professor's instructions naming us so we would step on the little tiles at that moment.

"First The Bear, now me, your turn Agnux, and last Pasca."

The engravings sank under our feet, lowering a few centimeters, but we waited and waited and nothing happened.

"Damn, I made a childish mistake, I confused the waxing moon with the waning moon! Get ready again."

We input the new sequence and the enormous slab sealing the door slid upward opening it. There it was, it was the way out of this bubble. We were all dumbfounded.

"Let's go boys, let's get moving!" exclaimed the old man who was already near the huge door.

We all ran toward the exit. The Bear lagged behind and when he got off his tile the door started lowering. We raced at full speed; I thought we wouldn't make it. Alb waited for us at the door trying to stop the enormous slab somehow, but there was no way. The man, who was the slowest in the group, arrived late, when we were all trying to hold up the massive stone sheet.

"Come on, come on, go now! I'll handle it!"

It was unbelievable, he was holding the door up alone. Then I understood the meaning of his name.

We crawled through the opening while the man held it with all his might. It was barely a crack now and finally it sealed shut making the ground tremble with its enormous weight. That was the last time we saw The Bear.

WE NEEDED TO VERIFY that we were right: that it was possible to mark space and see how time acts on it. The results would have to confirm that time is not uniform as we perceive it; instead, it is formed by a conglomeration of waves, more resembling a raging sea.

A motorized vehicle, possibly a motorcycle, due to the rough terrain, should travel quickly in a straight line from point A to B, releasing an ionized gas contained in a high pressure cylinder. At point A, a laser marker will send a beam of light through the vaporized ether in the air. The ray of light should become distorted, displaying the curvatures of space-time.

I had tossed and turned in bed all night; I must have dreamed about the test at least a hundred times that night. Finally the alarm clock started chiming its brass bells. I wanted to jump up, but as soon as I sat up my head started spinning. I made a good breakfast, though my stomach seemed to shrink by the minute. With great effort I managed to eat the eggs with bacon, but they kept churning in my guts; I felt like a washing machine. I arrived at the meeting point on my old bicycle. It was a sturdy machine, one they didn't make anymore, a gift from my father when I turned sixteen. My father was a very practical man, this way he saved my bus fare and forced me to exercise, something my legs have been very thankful for.

"Good morning professor." The young soldier guarding the fence gate told me.

"Good morning, Thomas."

The entire perimeter of the field where the experiment would take place was fenced off and cordoned by the army. I started taking out my ID card, but the young man quickly opened the barrier to let me through. I continued pedaling down the gently sloping yellow gravel path leading to the temporary sheds we used as a laboratory. Normally, everything tended to be very peaceful, but today was the big day and that placid spot amidst the green hills looked like a military drill field; soldiers were arriving and taking up positions everywhere. We had been working at that site for nearly two years, and although it was a high security area given the secrecy with which the government was handling the matter, the place tended to be very calm, except for the few occasions when the board of directors, "the big fish," visited us, asking vague questions and paying scarce attention to what we were doing there. "Reviewing, making appearances, to justify their salaries."

The tests with the motorcycle transporting the gas cylinder didn't yield good results. The rough terrain and poor consistency of the ground due to high moisture, sank the tires into the dirt, with mud covering half the rim. They were gorgeous machines, twin-cylinder 750 cc bikes straight out of the factory. The army was sparing no expense. After trying it over land they tried it by air; however, even though the pilot was very skilled, we couldn't trace the vapor trail low enough and parallel to the ground. Finally, we opted for a cable, a winch capable of supporting a man's weight, that the device dispersing the ether would slide down like a cable car.

I looked at my pocket watch; there were two little lines left for the minute hand to complete the circle. In 10 minutes we'd have just enough time to get everything ready and be able to fire the laser.

The colonel and his entourage of subordinates formed a standing grandstand in their ridiculous brand new white lab coats. They looked from side to side with their binoculars. From afar they looked like a family of meerkats.

I raised the green flag and it waved at precisely the moment I should lower it to signal the start of the test. I held my breath while watching that piece of cloth, which wouldn't stop flapping vigorously. In over thirty days I hadn't seen a single leaf move in the valley. It had been very difficult to select the site, in fact we only found one other place with similar characteristics and it was on the other side of the world, in a remote spot in Asia. I felt an itch in my throat; my nerves had left my mouth dry and I had trouble swallowing. How was this possible? Why does everything that can go wrong, go wrong at the last minute? With that wind it was impossible to form a uniform cloud and the measurements wouldn't be conclusive. When I was turning purple, I was able to exhale and breathe again, because the flag stopped moving. I enthusiastically lowered my arm, signaling as planned for the start of the test. My young assistant pulled the cord that activated the release mechanism. The gondola with the cylinder slid down quickly releasing its contents. When the first one reached the center of the ravine, I would have to release the opposite one, which would descend the same cable. Stage one arrived perfectly at point zero and I pulled my rope unlatching the second one. It started descending. Its acceleration was progressive. Then a strange sound was heard, like a violin string breaking. After that, a metallic thud and the cable car came to an abrupt stop. The cable swung so hard it nearly tore off the turret securing it. This couldn't be happening, I put my hand to my face covering my mouth, so I wouldn't utter some vulgarity...

I didn't have time for complex solutions, so I hopped on my bike, went up to the cable car that was stuck right at the start of the descent, grabbed the cylinder, put it on my back and took off down the slope without thinking twice. The stones on the path made the wheels bounce so much I spent more time in the air than on the ground. My old Gazelle absorbed the shocks, sliding downhill at full speed. I glanced back and saw I was managing a fairly uniform line with the gas; the test was a success, the laser passing through it formed undulations. We were actually right: space and time weren't rigid, they were in constant flux, like the ocean's surface. I let out a laugh of happiness: my theories were finally confirmed.

"Watch out Alb!"

I heard my assistant yell and when I looked ahead I saw a huge pine tree in my path. I couldn't do anything except close my eyes tightly. I felt weightless; I opened my eyes; I thought I was a bird, but the flight was brief; gravity quickly took over and I banged my head spending a week in the hospital.

TRAVELING BY CAR WITH him was torture, worse than a toothache; when he drove no one dared contradict him, for fear of having to walk home. So The Bear took advantage of this circumstance to tell outlandish tales, real bragging that increased since the listeners had to play along if they wanted to continue the trip. He became increasingly full of himself, I don't know a more blustering man. All his conversations revolved around sex, and of course, according to him he was not only a smooth operator but a lovemaking machine. Not only were the things he recounted ridiculous, when told by a person like him with his diminished physical attributes, they made him a pathetic character. How could a man his age brag about hooking up with underage girls? He wasn't satisfied with boasting about it, he also had to provide details of the situation, which produced an acidic feeling in one's stomach reflected by the facial muscle contractions of the listeners. I don't know, I guess The Bear didn't know how to read people's facial expressions very well, because when he saw this tension his obscenities increased as if the audience was enjoying his words.

WHENEVER I JUMP FROM one bubble to another, I feel heavy in the stomach and dizzy in the head. Fortunately I don't throw up easily and manage to recover quickly. But our friend Pasca doesn't seem to handle it as well and has been on his knees for several minutes expelling everything in his stomach.

The floor was made of a material like glass; the walls and ceiling were also transparent. It was curious; out of the corner of your eye they didn't look like it. When you looked straight on you could see the amazing structure. You could see through it, and the light seemed to come from wherever you looked. On the other hand, any other place you didn't look was dark. I could see the differences by concentrating on peripheral vision. I realized the walls here were different, they weren't transparent and seemed to be made of solid metal. It had to be an intelligent surface. Somehow the tubular structure of those corridors seemed to know where I was looking and turned on the light in that spot, so to speak.

Alb had taken off the jacket of his suit and was carrying it folded over one arm. The dirty, wrinkled shirt, the loosened tie. He was wearing his socks pulled up to his knees, over the hem of his pants. His appearance reminded me of my grandfather many years ago, when he used to ride a bicycle. The rest of the team was much less presentable.

"Have you noticed the structure? It's colossal. It has to be a construction far ahead of our time," commented the professor, running his palm over his head, trying to smooth his hair a bit that way.

"I'd say this looks more like the work of an extraterrestrial civilization."

Pasca thought like me, although he didn't give many explanations; it was clear we had both seen and read a lot on the subject. Something very curious happens with science fiction, just put one of these movies on for my mother and observe her commentary. She doesn't question the plot: some green beings coming in a flying hubcap crossing the vastness of the universe should give them an intelligence light years ahead of ours, and when they arrive on Earth they breathe our air, eat our food, and what's more, they like our food. They even like the girls on Earth, even though they look nothing like them; but what's most curious is that when they land they become quite stupid, dumber than us; and as always, we humans make their lives impossible... Well, what I was getting at is that she doesn't doubt any of this, detracting credibility; then, for example, in one scene she sees a character picking a lock with a paper clip and says: What a stupid movie! Who would believe you can open a door with a piece of wire?

Alb replied:

"I know it was built by humans by the height of the hallways, the breathable air inside, the ideal temperature for man and above all by the inscription right under our feet."

We all looked at the floor, none of us had noticed the huge inscription right below us: "United Nations Organization."

The hallways were marked, though not in the way we're accustomed to. You thought about where you wanted to go and a virtual sign appeared, a holographic arrow floating in the air pointing the way. I'm not too sure about the type of technology this machine used. I think somehow the ship's computer could read our thoughts and insert images into our brains. I deduced this because the arrow was only seen by the person thinking about it, and the light illuminating the corridors with our gaze wasn't perceived by the others either.

"Let's all think about the bridge, the place the ship is controlled from."

We walked following those indications floating in the air and arrived at a circular room. But some things were missing in this enclosure; in movies there are always multitudes of panels with buttons and levers everywhere. We also didn't find the typical computers full of colored lights. Instead, in the center of the room there were a few circles raised about four inches off the surface. They didn't even have seats. Maybe interstellar travel didn't need them? What does it matter if you stand or sit when the trip lasts thousands of years?

The professor got onto one of these circles and stood rigid; he seemed to have lost consciousness. A noise was heard like an electric motor starting up. The room started vibrating and the old man came out of his trance, trembling, and had to sit on the floor to recover.

"The machine has the capacity to transport people through space-time, but the computer is damaged and to open a bridge between the departure point and arrival point you have to perform all the calculations mentally, without making the slightest error, continuously adjusting as only a supercomputer can do. It needs to constantly receive the parameters that keep the wormhole open since points A and B are moving through space-time..."

"I'll try it!" Pasca exclaimed, climbing onto one of the circles.

Again, when he got on, the same thing happened to him: he stiffened, as if a strong electric current ran through his body. The start-up noise was heard again. He began to see complicated digits flying around him. He focused on those numbers; since childhood he'd had a special skill with math: if he made an effort he saw numbers as geometric figures and found the answer to any equation instantly, since he was able to view the result as an image instead of a series of numbers. The floor started shaking and then a sort of blur appeared on two of the circles distorting the space.

"It's unbelievable; to achieve this Pasca has to be performing endless calculations per second."

"I can't take it anymore, get in now!" he shouted, and that's what we did.

Alb and I managed to get out of the bubble, but our friend Pasca, Chapas, as they called him when he was little, also nicknamed Brasas during the years he spent locked up in a psychiatric hospital, remained lost in that strange place.

THE FLUORESCENT TUBES emitted a low quality white light, denoting the countless hours of use. The lighting and the fact I didn't see or hear anyone, made the place seem cold and inhospitable. A subway station, where the comings and goings of passengers is incessant, becomes a unique place when no one is there.

How big could this bubble be? From what I had seen so far, they could be as small as a room or immensely huge to contain a city inside.

Time wasn't on my side, I hadn't kept a very tight calculation since separating from the group I had given up everything as lost. The professor kept good track of the time we had left, and I only made a vague approximation.

I saw someone familiar at the end of the platform: could it be her? Without looking at me she disappeared walking into the darkness of the underground. I didn't think about it for an instant, I took off after her. Once away from the station, the darkness was total; I know the professor would have advised me against running through the tunnels, wasting the little time we had left. The most sensible thing would be to look for the exit from this sphere as soon as possible. But what if it was her?

I completely forgot everything and ran after her. Barely a few meters into the tunnel and the light completely disappeared, I found myself moving through total darkness.

AFTER THE EXHAUSTIVE interrogation they subjected Leon to, they managed to get little clarity. The man didn't know how he had gotten to the school, he was supposed to make a delivery, some boxes he was carrying in his truck. When he arrived he found everything deserted, but fortunately as he tells it, he found a treasure in the kitchen, a whole box of bottles of anise liquor and not just any liquor, they were his favorite brand, the best in the whole world. He drank until he lost consciousness and since there were many empty beds he spent the night in one of them; then, for breakfast, he made himself a good glass of Sanblas and continued the party. Outside it was very cold so he put on the NBC suit to go take a look at the generator. A task he was just now returning from, which he hadn't carried out due to lack of fuel, not the generator's fuel, but his own fuel, so he went back in for another bottle. That was all. He didn't know anything else.

"We have to get out of this bubble!" said the injured man in a weak voice. Everyone looked at him.

"Whaat's that kid sayin'! Is he drunnk or whaat?"

The patient had lost a lot of blood. The operation seemed to be going well, with all the assistants helping in one way or another. His pulse began dropping and his heart stopped beating.

"Don't die... come on, fight a little, come on, 1001, 1002, breathe," Kira yelled while performing resuscitation maneuvers on him. She pressed forcefully on his chest with her hands and gave him mouth-to-mouth.

The boy suddenly opened his eyes and abruptly inhaled, as if he'd been holding his breath for minutes. Then he continued breathing slowly and his eyelids were closing again. So the doctor held his face with her hands to lift him up.

"Look at me, don't close your eyes, make an effort. Come on!, come on!, let's go!. You have to stay conscious. What's your name?"

The young man tried to speak but nothing could be heard. She moved closer so he could whisper in her ear. He murmured something the others couldn't make out.

(I'm sure you remember this scene) But Kira was able to understand those words: "I'm Agnux we have to get out of this bubble."

"We have to deactivate the machine, we have to turn it off to get out of this sphere," the young man spoke again, louder, sitting up.

How much time had passed? Kira wondered. She couldn't remember; all her recollections were very confusing. It was possible days or even weeks had gone by since the accident. The patient was showing incredible recovery and his wounds had taken time to heal.

He got to his feet with difficulty and explained, to the listeners' astonishment, what was happening. They were trapped in an alternate reality, a piece of space-time kidnapped from its place of origin. The story seemed taken from a science fiction novel, but the evidence he referred them to over and over completely confirmed the theory. The machine was located in the old underground tunnels they had accidentally crossed, in that dark, damp place where the beast lived. That thing was responsible for the mess. Scientists in the mid-20th century produced a tear in the fabric of the universe opening the doors to another dimension. Part of the staff in charge of carrying out the experiment disappeared, swallowed up by the opening; in turn, something managed to get out. It adapted to our world, surviving in the tunnels of the old laboratory complex. The staff who managed to survive never spoke of the subject again. The underground was sealed off and no one ever returned to that place. That dark being had plenty of time to learn how the machine worked and took care of supplying it with power, managing to steal fragments of our world, portions of varying sizes sealed in bubbles. I've had to go through multitudes of these inert worlds, always pursued by mushy things. Thanks to the help of some good people who assisted me along the way. Now we're at the center, we have to go and disconnect the. The main entrance is in the old subway station near 43rd street.

"If it's about saving the world once more, me and my truck are at your complete disposal."

They all ran to the truck; the policeman begged Leon to let him drive, but he didn't accept.

"At least don't drink and drive at the same time. We definitely won't make it out of this one."

They took off bouncing around; the ancient truck picked up speed wheezing and blowing steam from the front of the hood.

"Onward Rocinante, we ride again like old times, on a mission to save the Earth!"

The truck zigzagged down the avenue, swerving from side to side, somehow managing to dodge all obstacles. Not even the best specialist, the most experienced pilot would be capable of performing the feats that alcoholic was carrying out at the wheel. It had no logical explanation. Phil and the guard stared at him fixedly while he drove. The man was barely watching the road and instead of gripping the huge steering wheel firmly he leaned on it, resting his elbows and forearms; he just slumped over it. They reached a spot where the street was blocked off; the ground had given way again forming an enormous pit.

"Brake! Stop or we'll kill ourselves!"

"Buckle up, we're taking off!"

To this day no one has been able to reasonably explain what happened. The driver took advantage of part of the sidewalk, along with some rubble piles as a ramp and managed to make the junk heap fly through the air, crossing the enormous ditch. The truck bounced several times on landing and lost part of the body, a side mirror, the bumpers and several other elements, but continued on unperturbed.

"And you wanted to miss this!"

They sped down the street at full speed and Leon decided to take a swig of anise while driving. Phil tried to hold onto the steering wheel to guide the truck, dodging obstacles, while the driver calmly reclined in his seat, leaning back. The policeman covered his eyes with his hands.

"But! What the hell? Are you drunk?"

"Buckle up, we're taking off!" he said, braking abruptly and swerving the wreck across the middle.

An elderly white-haired man came out of nowhere, riding a bicycle at full speed. Although he properly crossed, performing all the old-fashioned driving maneuvers, signaling with his arm and ringing the bell to indicate turning, the truck driver, focused on his bottle, hadn't seen him and nearly ran him over. The man dressed in an old plaid suit matching his jacket, lost control of his bike from the scare. The handlebars shook and he lost control, crashing into some trash cans. They all hurriedly got out of the truck to see what had happened and the man emerged from the garbage, dusting off his suit.

"Alb! Is that you?"

"Who's talking? Boy! My old friend, we meet again..."

The professor had made it through the spheres; truthfully he thought he'd never see him again. Both seemed visibly moved by the encounter and they hugged tightly. They got back in the truck and immediately managed to arrive at the old station.

"Stay here everyone, this is a problem I'm responsible for and I'm the one who has to go down there."

"Alb I won't let you go alone!"

"My old friend Agnux, always willing to help me. Let me tell you a little legend: Many years ago I had an idea: I thought space-time wasn't static, that time and matter itself are much more fickle than they seem. We prepared a huge experiment that has been rumored about for many years: the Philadelphia Project. Yes, you know some of the story but you're missing a few pieces to complete the puzzle, my dear friend. Doesn't it strike you as odd that from day one you found me familiar, that you had knowledge about the project, without me telling you anything?"

Then the old man took his wallet from the inside pocket of his jacket and extracted an old photo showing a group of scientists in their white lab coats.

"Take a look at the young man right next to me on my right."

Then all the memories returned to my mind, as if waking from a long trance. I was one of the scientists who disappeared in the experiment and had been lost all those years wandering through those bubbles. Alb was the project director, my boss, professor, and above all colleague. He had crossed the singularity to bring back the lost members of the laboratory. Now I understood everything; the main mission was to disconnect the machine and stabilize the planet. If we turned off that artifact everything would return to normal and each of us would go back to where we belonged.

The subway entrance was darker than a wolf's mouth.

"Waaait, I'm comin' with you! Maybe I'm a scientist too!" the truck driver yelled, approaching with a flashlight in hand.

And so the three of us went down the steps until we reached the entrance. I pushed the door and a warm breeze smelling of sewer welcomed me abruptly. The old subway museum was located in the underground, and inside one of the ancient metal doors, oxidized by years, connected to the archaic laboratory tunnels. How would we open that door? I wondered, but before I could say anything the professor took out a brass key that hung from the chain of his pocket watch.

"I hope this access still works, it's been many years since it was used."

The key fit perfectly into the lock and surprisingly moved the gears without any problem, but when we tried to open it, the door didn't budge. I helped pull it but nothing, it seemed as if it had been welded shut.

"Let me, let's see! It must be stuck!"

He gave it two good kicks and a large amount of ochre dust came off the frame. Then with just lightly pulling on the knob the door slid, but halfway it got stuck again, this time due to the tiles. The stench coming from inside made you retch. We went in covering our mouths with our hands, but good old Leon didn't even flinch, he took a swig from his canteen, sloshed the liquor around his mouth, licked his lips and finally wiped his mouth on his shirtsleeve. We walked for quite a while through narrow tunnels, passing countless intersections where various branches converged; the place was a real maze, but my friend walked with purpose, without hesitating for an instant about which corridor to take. Finally we arrived at a large room; the place was filled with some ancient computers, the size of closets, lined up like an army of neatly aligned soldiers. The site was covered in dust and cobwebs and it brought back some memories; yes, I was certain I had worked in that place. Although now the place was cold and eerie, in full operation back in the day, with all the staff, it had almost seemed cozy.

TOMORROW WE HAVE A doctor's appointment; I'll try by all means to convince him to run some tests and detect her illness, while there's still time.

I've carried out all kinds of tests and there's no way to alter events. The other day, at the supermarket, I filled my pockets with candy bars; that way, when I went through the security gate the alarm would sound and the script of my life would be disrupted, changing history. But when I went through checkout nothing happened, the alarm didn't go off and I tried going through several times but nothing. I put my hands in my pockets to take out the chocolates, but they were empty. The candy seemed to have instantly jumped from my pocket to its rightful place on the candy shelf.

I RACED UP THE STAIRS of that building. My leg muscles burned from the effort. I could clearly hear my breathing, but there was no echo, as if the walls of the structure absorbed sounds. The stairs zigzagged, back and forth, constantly making me change direction. To climb faster, I grabbed onto the railing and took advantage of all the available space, turning it into a spiral run. After running for a few minutes, I started feeling dizzy. There were no doors, rooms, or landings; just rows of steps one after another. I brought my head close to the railing and I could look down through the stairwell, seeing the great height I was at and the number of floors I had climbed. I took a breath trying to catch my breath and looked up with my head against the structure to see how much I had left to reach the top floor. I saw I didn't have much farther, three or four more flights, and a relieved smile formed on my face.

It was vitally important to get out of this bubble as soon as possible; I don't know how long I'd been lost, but what was very clear was that there wasn't much time left. I figured the top floor must have access to the roof, and from there I would probably be able to get out of the sphere. I ran again, encouraged by how little was left to reach the top floor. Jumping two steps at a time, I continued to the last floor. I turned one last time, leaning on my hands, and my face paled when I saw the steps embedded in a wall. It made no sense, it was as if they had sealed off the hallway where the stairs went up. I got closer to examine the wall more closely, looking for cracks or crevices. I thought it might be a false wall and maybe I could knock it down with a push. The wall, the same white color as the rest of the stairs, was cold as a block of ice. I tapped it with my hands; it seemed solid as granite. Still, I rammed it a few times with my shoulder, throwing my whole body against it. Impossible, it didn't work. Who would design this building? It wasn't a normal structure, it seemed taken from a nightmare. I didn't have much time, so I started going back down as fast as I could. At least going down was quite a bit less tiring and more fun, since I jumped from almost the middle of each flight of steps, hands forward to grab the railing bar and swing from my arms to turn. I was definitely taking much less time going down, although with so many turns I was starting to get dizzy. I jumped from a step earlier than usual and could barely grab onto the bar. My heart skipped a beat, if I hadn't caught it, I would have fallen headfirst down the stairs. When I looked forward, still holding on, I encountered another wall in the middle of the staircase. What was happening? How could such a building be constructed? Roughly calculating, it turned out I had descended fewer floors than I had climbed, so something very strange was going on here.

A low humming grew louder, becoming deafening noise; then the floor under my feet started vibrating. The wall seemed to be moving toward me. The hallway was shrinking and its walls were getting closer and closer together. I ran back upstairs again, while trying to find a logical explanation for what was happening. Was it possible the bubble was shrinking? Something must be causing instability. One way or another, I'd have to hurry up and leave this place if I wanted to live to tell about it. I ascended as fast as my legs would allow. For the moment I was a good number of floors ahead of the distortion. I changed direction again to face the new stretch of steps and I was surprised again. What should have been a new stretch of ascending staircase became descending, taking me back down to the previous floor. A sort of space-time loop prevented me from moving forward. I leaned out again over the stairwell and I could see the distortion continuing to rise, eliminating everything in its path.

"Wait a minute! You have to think of something."

Where was the light coming from? The stairs were lit up, but the ceiling had no bulbs. I looked toward the light and saw a sort of skylight on each half-landing: a rectangular hole in the wall, as deep as a niche. I jumped in head first. My feet were left hanging out in the hallway, and

I could see the exterior through a barred window. The bars didn't look too sturdy. They were staggered, one up and down and the next down and up, with the ends shaped like spear points, not quite touching the ceiling. I tried bending them with my hands, gripping them tightly at the tip; I managed to move one a bit, but it was too sturdy to bend. So I went back out to the stairs to turn around; going in feet first I could kick the grate with more force. The hallway was crumbling, pieces of the ceiling were falling everywhere; the shaking was more pronounced, like an earthquake, and the sound was approaching. There wasn't much time left. I forcefully kicked the bar with my feet and it gave way a little. I landed a series of consecutive kicks and managed to bend it. With my head still in the stairwell, I could see the walls closing in on me. I slid down and was able to slip out between the bars onto the street. I breathed relieved for just a second, because I immediately saw I was hanging from the bars of that tiny window, at a considerable height from the ground. I must have been twelve or thirteen stories high, and the building's outer wall was smooth, concrete. There was nowhere to grab hold, I looked to the other side and found a bundle of cables running down the wall. I held on tightly and prayed they wouldn't break under my weight. I started climbing down the facade and with each step I felt more secure and confident.

In this bubble there was no wind; in fact the air was scarce and stale, like a house closed up for years. I looked down. I didn't have much farther and surveyed the place. I had to quickly figure out the situation. Where would the exit be?

In the distance, at the end of the street I thought I saw something move. I kept descending without taking my eyes off the street, and again something crossed under the marquees. It was almost certainly a person. I didn't know how many more individuals I would encounter, each sphere was a complete mystery. A sort of puzzle to be solved, in an attempt to get back home.

I didn't have many meters left to reach the ground and again someone ran across the street; almost right under my feet. In the space between buildings, I was able to see her in more detail.

"Heyyy! Up here!" I yelled loudly to get her attention. She stopped for an instant and looked at me. I couldn't believe my eyes, it was definitely her. There was no doubt, in the subway tunnels I couldn't be certain, the dim light made it very difficult to identify her; but now, in broad daylight there was no doubt. My heart started beating hard and I hurried down the last meters I had left.

Could it be her? Yes, I'm sure she was wearing the red dress I gave her. Yes, I think there's no doubt. She's probably confused. Almost certainly, she was the person I had seen several times. She must be disoriented, maybe she thought she was in a dream. At first, it took me a long time to get my bearings; everything was blurry, out-of-focus images.

If it hadn't been for Alb I probably would still be lost in the first bubble, that's best case scenario. Surely Kira has been following me unconsciously, I seem familiar to her and that's why she's passed through several spheres after me. I didn't stop running and asking myself questions until I managed to turn the corner. There she was, standing still, looking at me as if she didn't know me. She was wearing that pretty dress matching some flat shoes in the same color. I wanted to tell her so many things, I missed her so much, I had fantasized so many times about seeing her again. Fleeting dreams where she vanished like smoke between my arms. But now I was awake, and she was just steps away. Her pale face shone under the sunlight. Her lovely orange freckles colored her cheeks. Her wavy hair produced orange glints under that light.

I took a slow step, moving closer slowly and she did the same, stepping back, keeping her distance. I guess she was in shock. For her the situation must be very strange. Most likely she had been wandering for days if not months or even years, going from one bubble to another.

Who knows what difficulties she's had to face? How has she managed to survive? Luckily maybe she hasn't had to confront the wormoids. But all that didn't matter now, at last we were together again and nothing and no one would separate us. This time I wouldn't let her leave and I would follow her to the depths of hell itself if necessary.

I took another step, softly uttering her name so as not to frighten her. She looked at me intently, with a lost, dark gaze, as if she were catatonic. She took yet another step away from me. She staggered and fell. During this whole time I was only looking at her lovely face and didn't notice the cavity opening under her feet. The street was split, cleanly cut, and then it fell into an abyss into the depths of the earth. This bubble was very unstable and it seemed a piece of road had been swallowed up. My heart nearly jumped out of my mouth when I saw her fall into the precipice. I ran with all my might and jumped in head first, trying to grab her hands as she slid down the asphalt slope leading to the deep crevice. I managed to grab her firmly by the arms, but I couldn't stop her fall; now, we both slid down the smooth pavement slope. Despite the pain caused by the friction of the asphalt on my body, I clung to it with all my might to brake our fall. But I only managed to slightly reduce the speed.

I couldn't believe what was happening: in such a short period of time I had found Kira again and now I was about to lose her once more. But now I knew the pain this entailed. I would rather die with her than keep living alone. Long ago the idea of dying came to me as an end to my suffering, as a deserved rest after so much work. If it hadn't been for the possibility of changing the course of history by altering the order of events in the script our cosmic clock ceaselessly wrote, if it hadn't been for the thought of managing to change the past, I wouldn't continue filling my lungs with air. Filling my blood with oxygen, so my broken heart could keep pumping life into my body. A shattered cardiac muscle that suffered with each beat. I wouldn't let her fall in any way. I shouted in anger, in fury, digging my hands into the street, clinging on with my nails. My fingers bled but I felt no pain, only rage. Powerlessness at that situation. This wasn't about Kira and me, it wasn't about that damned bubble or the fucking abyss we were heading to; this was something personal, between God and me. As if that supreme being delighted in putting me in trouble, it seemed he had no other entertainment than watching me suffer. But even if I was just a tiny ant and he a titanic colossus, I had to stick to him, biting him in fury for all eternity. Finally we reached the very edge of the pit and I managed to grab on tightly to some rusty iron bars jutting from the asphalt. With the other hand I held her as she dangled over the endless black depths of that precipice.

"Don't worry sweetheart, I won't leave you alone again."

Those were my words. She became heavier and heavier, and if it was already hard for me to climb up on my own, I don't know how I'd manage to pull her up. She seemed to weigh a ton. I looked at her face to reassure her, but her gaze remained dull, dark, as if her eyes had no life. The skin on her face seemed to wrinkle, as if it were made of fine cloth and something was moving underneath it. Then it burst open and a jumble of black worms came out of her interior. Her whole body decomposed, transforming into a black tangle of worms. I let go of her hand, but in the fall it managed to adhere to my legs. I tried to shake off that disgusting mess of worms. I held on tightly with both hands to the metal ledge and kicked forcefully at that shapeless, foul-smelling mass. It covered my legs, trying to devour me, taking on the shape of a giant leech. It was the most repugnant thing I could imagine. I kicked with all my might, as if shooting a ball to take a penalty kick; with each blow I managed to rip off a chunk of fleshy mass. I kept battering it as if my life depended on it, and indeed it did. The wormoid seemed to weaken and it started making a frightful sound, like a phlegmy, raspy scream. Finally, I managed to shake it off and it fell into the darkness of that deep hell, disappearing into the distance without stopping its horrifying sound. I swung back and forth; gathering momentum I managed to bring my right leg up to the height of my hands; then, with effort I succeeded in clambering up and ascending the pavement. I climbed very carefully up the inclined street, which, given its slope was more like a wall. Thanks to my practiced friction climbing technique, distributing my body weight between arms and legs and taking advantage of the slightest protrusion, I climbed until reaching the top of the damned ramp.

During this whole time I kept thinking about what had happened. What was going on? Was I going crazy? My feelings clashed, my brain seemed like a battlefield, some neurons battling others. Feelings of sadness, relief, anger, disgust, all at the same time and mixed together. Somehow, the wormoids, that shapeless rotten mass, seemed to be learning new tactics. Somehow they had entered my dreams and copied Kira's image. They were able to mimic and take on her form, they even had the ability to act like a human being.

A peculiarity in the bubble's membrane showed the bridge to the next one. The bad thing was it was on the other side of the precipice. It was time to get out of this place, without wasting any more time. On the street there were parked cars on both sides, and in the middle, some vehicles that must have been sucked in by the sphere while moving down the avenue. Perfect! I thought when I saw a high-powered sports car. The keys were in it; as soon as I turned the ignition the engine roared to life angrily. I never pictured myself driving a touring car.

I floored the accelerator, keeping the brake pressed at the same time as I released the clutch pedal and the wheels started sliding on the asphalt, heating up and burning the tires from the friction. When the tachometer needle reached the start of the red line I released the brake and the car shot out like a bullet into the abyss.

The Complex

UNDERGROUND THERE WAS a veritable maze, room after room connected by long corridors; moldy walls on which you could see the moisture climbing from the bottom in the form of dark stains devouring the paint. Underground chambers without any ventilation, stale air, dense sweetish strong odor. The lighting was only partial since the entire complex was designed to be used by a single person; so when the light in one hallway turned on it automatically turned off in the previous one. This lighting in sections left you lost in the enormous stretches of the corridors, enveloped by a threatening darkness that seemed to lurk behind you. The cold fluorescent tubes glimmered and clicked when connected, for brief instants, while the previous section turned off and the new one turned on, everything was left in absolute darkness. Your breathing was cut off during that brief portion of time, making you doubt whether the next stretch of lamps would be able to turn on, because if that happened, it would be very difficult for someone unfamiliar with the complex in detail to find their way out in the dark.

The Death of Agnux's Father

I REMEMBER THE LAST time I saw my father. It was in the hospital, after his surgery. He had already been on the ward for several days and seemed to be out of danger. But the rest of the family didn't think so. I found him perfectly fine; I was sure he would recover. I always pictured being able to sense these sorts of things. But the truth is I didn't notice anything at all. He seemed as solid as a rock and the next morning they called me with the news of his passing. Life is much more complex than we imagine. Maybe we base many of our thoughts on hazy memories that aren't real, maybe based on movie scenes or passages from novels; be that as it may, one is always caught off guard by harsh reality.

I often wonder who writes our scripts, who chooses our fates. Do we really have control over our lives? I picture life as an absurd movie, in which there doesn't have to be heroes or villains, just people. Normal, ordinary people who go through their brief time like leaves drifting on an immense sea. Maybe it's all a sham, a sort of theatrical performance, maybe everyone is acting. I look at myself and look at them, we're not so different. People struggle to stand out and differentiate themselves from one another; but in reality we seem repetitive. Maybe four or even five, five different souls, occupying all human bodies. Just five basic molds to fill so many wrappers.

What is our destiny? What is our purpose? Most of us simply pass through life without leaving a trace, like a breath of wind, a whisper left forgotten. Are we just puppets in a performance, for the purpose of entertaining some superior being? But the more I try to grasp how our reality works, the more baffled I become. Although this also leads me to new assumptions. Since the gears that spin this cosmic web we call time are so complex, the solution must also be very complex. Possibly an endless path, on which to continually learn from our mistakes.

"IT'S THIS WAY, YES; going down through this hatch we'll reach the nerve center."

We lifted the grate on the floor and climbed down with difficulty through the opening. I held on tightly to the vertical ladder, carefully not to fall. When Alb and I were below it was our companion's turn, and seeing how clumsily he positioned himself on the first rung we expected the worst. He climbed down hesitantly, having trouble finding the next step and suddenly he came down on us. Luckily, he didn't have far to reach the ground and we were able to catch him, albeit not without effort: that man weighed a ton.

"Thanks, boy! You saved my life," he told me, speaking into my ear, leaning on my shoulder. The smell of anise on his breath nearly made me lose consciousness.

"Now we have to be very careful; to reach the core of the machine we have to pass near the magnetron nucleus. We have to stay as far away from it as we can. Leave all the metal objects you're carrying here and walk as close as possible to the tunnel wall. The power of this magnet is so strong that a single coin in your pocket would drag us toward it."

He left his watch, a pen and some coins on the ground, I also did the same and Leon left some things too. In this room we didn't need a flashlight, the device emitted a red light that covered everything. Dragging our backs along the cement we started to pass about fifteen feet from the device; it made a deafening noise, like throwing rocks in a washing machine.

"Hey, hey, let go, you oaf, let go of that!"

Although the man's intentions were good, I was starting to think we shouldn't have brought him along. What made us think he would part from his stainless steel canteen containing that liquor? He had hidden it under his shirt, thinking that way the magnetism wouldn't affect it and now he was being dragged toward it since it was tied to his belt. I tried to grab his hand, but I only managed to catch his shirt; the worn fabric ripped, leaving a piece in my hands. The man literally flew until he was embedded in an enormous cylinder several meters in diameter. He looked like a sticker stuck there motionless. He tried to break free, but the magnetic force was so strong he couldn't budge.

"Take off your belt, get rid of the flask!"

"Oh my God no, not my bottle, I'll die of thirst!"

He had no choice but to leave his canteen there. I never saw him so distraught, I think he even shed a tear.

We entered the gigantic vaulted room that housed the heart of the machine. Electrical conduits and water pipes fed and cooled the monster. We were under Independence Square. The old fountain supplied the liquid needed to maintain the proper operating temperature. It was a colossal work of art camouflaged right in the city center. Its core shone like a star, giving off tremendous heat.

"There's no time to lose, we have to disconnect the main cables, cutting off the power supply."

The hoses had connectors with multiple security devices. They were an alloy as shiny as gold, with alphanumeric rings engraved around them. The device worked like one of those combination lock chains used for securing bicycles, but much more complex and as thick as a fire hose. Alb positioned himself grabbing the connector near the core; I had to climb the cable to reach the terminal about sixty feet up on the dome.

"22-z to the right, 49-t to the left..."

That man proved to have a prodigious memory. He remembered all the sequences instantly and Agnux only had to adjust the rings following the instructions. The first umbilical cord came loose; when it released there was a loud pop and molten metal sparks fell like a fireworks flare lighting up the enormous room, going out when they hit the ground. The device lost power and its light dimmed. In the distance a frightful scream was heard coming from one of the tunnels. Then all kinds of voices were heard, insults and moans, both men's and women's, and even animal sounds. Whoever uttered them did so on the run, coming closer and closer.

"What are you doing, dogs? Stupid worms, don't touch my machine."

"Hurry, we only have one more left, reach the connector and let's input the code."

"Mama, mama, I think I peed myself..."

The sounds produced by that being were frightening, causing uncontrollable panic. It was approaching us at full speed and didn't seem to be in a good mood. Cutting off the power supply would return everything to normal and the monster wasn't happy about that one bit.

"08-r-23 left..."

I input the code as fast as I could and just before finishing an enormous worm-like creature came running into the room, black in color with appendages protruding everywhere, like the roots of a tuber. With one of those extremities it grabbed Leon by the ankles and started dragging him across the floor, taking him toward what looked like a huge mouth full of teeth. I heard a dull thud and the connector came loose, disconnecting from its socket. The thing started bellowing again, transforming back into that tall, empty-eyed man. It held the truck driver by the neck with one hand and opened its jaws again, showing crocodile-like fangs. The star-shaped core began expanding, the electric current confining it was cut off.

"Give me a hug, old friend!" he said, running toward the demon with arms outstretched. The blow freed Leon and made Alb and the monster fall into the glowing interior of the machine. The sphere exploded and an earthquake began to bring everything crumbling down. We raced toward the exit as fast as we could, but it was blocked by mounds of debris falling from the ceiling. The glass dome holding the fountain water cracked and the liquid came pouring in torrents; the water rose and by keeping afloat at the surface, we managed to reach the exterior. We came out through the fountain and everything had returned to normal. It was a sunny day and the chirping of birds could be heard throughout the square.

"Aren't you ashamed? Bathing in the fountain, a bunch of drunks..."

Were the words of a woman feeding pigeons, sitting on a park bench in the square.

I'M DRIVING WITH KIRA to the doctor's office. I remember this day perfectly. The doctor will joke about how few people get sick on Fridays. Then he'll write up some allergy prescriptions and finish the pad, having to go into the adjoining room for a new one. He'll say goodbye politely and we'll leave without further ado.

Prepared to repeat the scene again, I enter the waiting room, which is half empty. We patiently wait our turn and go in. There's the doctor, just as I remembered; he asks Kira some questions and I try to interrupt them over and over, but it seems like they're ignoring me. They continue with their roles without paying attention to anything I do or say. The desperation was such that I slapped the practitioner, breaking his glasses, but they immediately fixed themselves and they continued with the established script.

"Fridays there are always few people, it seems like everyone agrees to get sick on Mondays. Just a moment, my prescription pad ran out..."

This didn't look good at all, there's no worse punishment than knowing what's going to happen and not being able to do anything to prevent it. Then the doctor came back in; I was there with my head down looking at the floor.

"Well, here are the tests your wife needs to get!"

"What? What did you just say?"

That wasn't in the script; I looked up at the doctor, because I didn't believe what I had just heard. Alb occupied the doctor's chair, dressed in a white coat.

"I can't stay long, this is a blatant violation of the space-time continuum. With these papers they'll run tests on Kira and I'll add a report so they start treatment as soon as possible."

"See you soon old friend!"

He left the room, I went after him but when I opened the door, I found nothing but some people waiting for their turn.

Thoughts

OVER AND OVER, WHEREVER I look I see the same faces. Maybe four or five templates, four or five different molds, unique ones, that shaped all of us. Always the same ones repeated, identical like drops of water. I see myself reflected in their gazes when they laugh, when they cry, when they dream...

Do we really make our own decisions or do we simply follow the lines of an ancient script written since the beginning of time? I don't even know if I'm in control of my actions. How to know if any decision I make seems to require consultation? Yes, it's called reflecting, but who do I present the case to, with whom do I mentally discuss it until reaching a conclusion? If I'm just one person, why do I have to come to a consensus with myself before making a decision? Why do I have to wait for an inner voice to give me solutions to my problems?

I SLAMMED THE ACCELERATOR down, keeping the brake pressed while releasing the clutch pedal and the wheels started sliding on the asphalt, heating up and burning the tires from the friction. When the tachometer needle reached the start of the red line I released the brake and the car shot out like a bullet into the abyss.

The car landed on 43rd street; the asphalt was frozen and I lost control of the vehicle. I crashed head-on into a lamppost, the sports car was completely wrecked, but I hadn't suffered any injuries thanks to the airbags. I ran down the avenue, the wind was very strong.

But! How was it possible? On the opposite sidewalk was her. I carefully approached to check if it really was her. She was quite changed and dressed in an unusual way. I moved closer slowly, she looked at me but didn't recognize me. Could it be the Kira from another dimension? Either way I decided to find out. I walked crossing the intersection when I heard the squeal of brakes. Before I realized what was happening an SUV ran me over. The impact was tremendous and I fell to the ground losing consciousness.

TODAY A NEW DAY BEGINS and with it a new life. Dawn breaks and for the first time I don't know what will happen. The future for Kira and me is as unknown as it can be for anyone else. This uncertainty makes existence wonderful.

I've seen the very fabric of space-time, I've traveled through it, living infinite moments in an instant and watching a whole lifetime pass in the blink of an eye. Time is as fickle as water or wind. But if I've learned anything from all this, it's to enjoy every moment. To forget about time.

Appendix

Below you will find some of the scientific theories extracted from Agnux's works.

If you are not thinking about building a time machine, you don't need to read these pages.

The Refrigerator and the Time Machine

IF YOU'RE GOING TO travel through a wormhole, don't forget to dress warmly!

The theory of relativity formulated by Albert Einstein in 1905 changed how we see space and time, since the two joined together to form inseparable space-time. We were also able to confirm through the atomic bomb that matter contains a huge amount of energy. Thus now energy, mass and gravity were connected to form a perfect symbiosis. The theory of relativity stated that gravity could distort space-time forming a singularity: "black holes." Years later, observations confirmed the existence of these supermassive monsters that not even light can escape.

Could you travel through space-time by entering one of these singularities connected in a wormhole?

Inside this singularity, the enormous gravity eliminates all movement, matter is something like packets of energy; if we stop all movement there can be no heat emissions and the temperature should drop to absolute zero.

If you want to time travel economically, you can get in the fridge. "But I don't recommend it, you might ruin your mother's groceries."

Why Doesn't E.T. Call Home?

What does the failure of the SETI project tell us?

I remember not long ago when there was doubt about whether there were planets outside the solar system. Then came the big news: They found the first planet outside our system. Today not a day goes by when a new world isn't discovered. For a much longer time, the SETI project began its search for intelligent extraterrestrial life. Using the giant Arecibo radio telescope, signals from other civilizations were expected to be captured in a short time. But after the first year of searching: nothing, just silence. And in the following decade the search expanded, even I myself, along with millions of internet users, put our computers at the service of the exploration. Software processed the information gathered by radio telescopes on numerous computers around the world. And after the first decade of searching: nothing, just silence. The SETI project has been in operation for over 50 years and the results: zero.

Why doesn't E.T. call home?

At first I thought maybe we're very behind, that we're trying to communicate with The Flintstones. That our communication technology was very primitive.

I also thought maybe the supposed extraterrestrial civilizations are very private and don't want new friends.

But what if we're overlooking something? Maybe a physical law we're unaware of?

I think we continue to think in three dimensions and don't apply Albert Einstein's relativistic theories.

What if space could deform radio signals? If a uniform signal was fragmented and distorted...

Let's imagine a simple message: 1,2,3,4: if we receive this signal, we'll immediately know it's an intelligent signal. But what if when the signal travels through space it reaches us like this: 3,1,4,2, it would already be harder to interpret and detect. We've only introduced a slight variation and we no longer understand anything.

But time is much more complex. That's why in my novel I talk about nonlinear time, more complicated than a spiral model, like a skein, a ball of yarn. Imagine the signal sent: 1,2,3,4, arrived like this

Today:

Tomorrow: 1

Two years ago:

In five months:

• • • •

AND AS IF THIS WASN'T enough, the signal is received fragmented and each portion at a different frequency.

It's totally impossible to recognize a signal this random.

Will we never be able to communicate with other galaxies? Can signals arrive so encoded that we're unable to detect them?

But what if we aim at the point of emission and calculate what distortions the signal will suffer along its path, applying relativistic theories? Could we thereby have a sort of Rosetta Stone indicating when and at what frequency the messages would arrive?

The Speed at Which We Move

MATTER CANNOT TRAVEL at the speed of light, because its mass would become infinite. We observe that galaxies move, that the universe expands. Everything we perceive as matter is nothing more than packets of energy in motion that I call "vibration."

How to find a reference point to know at what speed we move?

Since everything depends on the reference point of the observer, we can.

We could take a hydrogen atom as a reference; if we could reveal the speed at which it vibrates, we could subtract this speed from that of light and find out what ours is.

Speed of movement through space = C speed of light - vibration speed of the energy packet that forms a hydrogen atom.

What is the True Passage of Time?

Is There a Universal Cosmic Clock?

There may be a mathematical formula that reveals the true passage of time on our planet.

It could be something like:

$T = G \bullet V2$

And by applying it we could decipher radio signals from another galaxy. Likewise, we could use it to know how gravity affects other planets or systems and thereby send a specific signal to each place.

Perhaps taking this into account, transmissions between Earth and the spacecraft we send to other worlds can be clearer and more secure.

$T = 300,000 \text{ km/s} = \text{Infinite time}$

$G = \text{force of gravity}$

$V = \text{Speed}$

How does mass affect time?

For example:

We take Earth's gravity = 1 • speed in space = Time

A Message in a Quantum

THE TINY PARTICLES that form the nucleus of an atom belong to it as if they had a serial number printed on them, something like a genetic code that only allows it to fit into its carrier. The small quantum particles are not tied to our timeline and by applying a small amount of energy to them they jump in time, always returning to their matrix. So we can take a few and keep them (in a jar), while their atoms are taken far away. When we wanted to send a message, we would give them energy and these particles would instantly jump from point A, the starting point, to point B, where the atom they belong to is located, traversing the fabric of space-time immediately. The particle has somehow fooled the laws of physics of our universe by making a journey faster than light. Like the thread that spins a cloth seems to jump at each stitch, but it's really an optical effect since we can't see the other side of the cloth. This is how the quantum particle fools space-time, traversing it to reach point B; it doesn't really move faster than light, but since it uses a shortcut it arrives sooner. In the hypothetical case that it could find its destination and move instantly, the following paradox would occur: the farther point A is from point B, the sooner the quantum would arrive, since moving faster than light, it would be traveling backwards in time. The particle would arrive even before departing.

THE CHANGEABLE PAST

WE ARE TRAPPED BY OUR senses. We can only perceive a timeline. A consecutive order of numbers that we form in our mind giving shape to time. But the passage of seconds is much more complex, we are unable to notice its fluctuations.

I wonder if yesterday was really yesterday, I look for some inconsistency in the events that happened. I know it's totally useless since it would be completely impossible for me to detect them. They could change our history for us, the most relevant data, and we would never realize it. Imagine we travel to the past and prevent Napoleon from being born; the very instant he would be erased from history forever and we ourselves would never remember he existed. He would suffer much more than a memory lapse, more than simple forgetting; it would be as if our entire existence was restructured. Everything would change all at once, but absolutely no one would notice; even if we ourselves were the ones who changed history we would remain ignorant.

The Machine

ALBERT EINSTEIN OPENED Pandora's box when he formulated his theory of relativity. In his day it was said that only 3 people in the world were capable of understanding it, and even Einstein himself joked that not even he understood it. Although many still think it's just a theory without foundation, today without it our technology would be impossible. A clear example can be seen in GPS. Satellites, using radio waves, through triangulation, can mark the exact position of the user. And where do the relativistic theories come into play? As Albert predicted, time is not unchanging, not even a second is the same length in two different places. It turns out time is tied to space and can be stretched or shrunk by the force of gravity. A satellite, being far from Earth, is distanced from its gravity, so time for it is different than time for the user on land. If the clocks on those satellites weren't adjusted, it would be impossible to determine the user's position without errors.

The machine was built based on this theory. To alter time within it, we needed to create a great gravitational force. As we know, gravity decreases with distance, so we would have to send the information as close as possible to the gravitational force. To increase the mass and therefore the gravitational force of an object, we need to accelerate it. The greater the speed, the more its size increases and the more it distorts the surrounding space-time. The problem with accelerating an object to such speeds requires an enormous amount of energy. On the other hand, Einstein postulates that light itself can create a distortion in space. We could say light is time itself, and it can curve itself. We needed to create a sort of thin tube of light, whose walls, formed by photons, had enough energy to bend a space-time as small as the size of a photon. The quantum would be shot through that microscopic conduit with the information. The information should then be received even before being sent. For this to be possible, it's assumed you have to exceed the speed of light, but as we see here, we've fooled the quantum particle, so that it doesn't surpass the speed of light yet manages to travel a greater distance in less time. This is because space is compressed inside the tube, due to the force of artificial gravity created by the movement of the particles forming it. A simple example that we're all surely familiar with is passing a fluid through a transparent hose: If we squeeze the rubber narrowing its interior we can observe how the liquid passes through that spot faster.

By altering the laser's power we can send that message to different time points. As long as the machine is connected, messages from the future can be received, so something surprising happened: as soon as we connected the machine, before even sending a single message, we kept receiving interference that we later discovered were messages we ourselves would send in the future. Now I know for sure we weren't prepared to face the consequences that experiment would entail.

The machine managed to fold space-time, but a feedback began creating folds on top of themselves, increasing the temporal distortion and creating a wormhole that wouldn't stop growing.

We didn't take into account that by sending a signal to the past, it wouldn't just travel the four known dimensions. What happened was the following: the device not only picked up our transmitted signal sending it back in time, it also absorbed pieces of space, encapsulating them like crystal spheres. But there's even more, since if we send a signal to the past, we have to take into account the point of emission and the point of reception. The transmitter is at a specific date and a specific place in space. As we know, the Earth rotates on its axis, around the Sun and our solar system, around our galaxy the Milky Way; and it goes on and on. So if the message is sent a few hours into the past, it has to be received where the Earth was at that moment which, adding up all the speeds, could give us millions of kilometers of distance from the point of emission. However, what happened was much more complex, since somehow an echo signal was received in the machine, as if somehow the particles had a numbering, a barcode identifying them with where they belonged in the universe, and when jumping in time they automatically knew where to place themselves. But as I said, it was an echo signal, since the particles seemed to have cloned themselves, giving readings at the same time in different places in the universe.

After countless hours of work, the team came to certainly outlandish conclusions due to a complexity of the universe that we couldn't even have imagined. If a person had a time machine, say in a DeLorean, and traveled in time, they would encounter the following dilemma: they would appear for example in 1950, but in the current place where Earth is now, so they would almost certainly find themselves floating in space, inside their sports car in the middle of nothing, in the 1950s, but where Earth is right now; our planet would therefore be light years away. Somehow, as I've said, every particle seems to be unique; like pieces of a puzzle, they only fit in their corresponding place. While one individual is left floating lost in space, another appears where they belong. "At least that's what happened with the information; we never believed it possible for anything larger than a quantum particle to jump in time, separating from the space-time it belonged to."

Elastic Space
Doppler Effect

WHEN THE WHISTLE OF an oncoming train sounds, we can hear a different sound than when it moves away. This is due to the compression of the waves. In the same way, this phenomenon was applied to light and, depending on the frequency at which the waves from a star reach us, we can know if it was approaching or moving away. But what really happens when a star moves away from us? As we reason according to our experiences, when a train moves away from us we simply see it advance along the tracks, moving across the land; we instinctively apply this idea to the galaxy moving away from us. But what if instead of moving through space, as the train shows us, what's happening is that the space between us is stretching? Think of a rubber band: if we hold each end with one hand and stretch it, the distance between the two hands increases, but the rubber remains the same...

Did you love *Kira and the Ice Storm*? Then you should read *Freak - The Circus of Horrors*[1] by Francisco Angulo de Lafuente!

Critics are hailing Francisco Angulo latest novel Freak as "a modern gothic masterpiece" (The New York Times) that is "impossible to put down" (Washington Post).

Set against the backdrop of a mysterious traveling circus, Freak chronicles the experiences of a group of extraordinary characters who possess uncanny abilities and physical anomalies that set them apart from mainstream society. Led by the enigmatic magician known only as "Nikola," the "freaks" of the circus unveil a riveting story of drama, suspense, romance, horror, and humanity.

As Angulo peels back the layers of his vividly drawn characters, he illuminates the struggles of those deemed abnormal and the cruelty

---

1. https://books2read.com/u/3nB8v6

2. https://books2read.com/u/3nB8v6

and wonder of human nature. Heart-wrenching, chilling and tender by turns, Freak explores discrimination, revenge, compassion and redemption with sensitivity and depth.

Hailed for its "spellbinding pace and tantalizing secrets" (Chicago Tribune), Freak conjures up a world that seduces readers into the rich inner lives of beings who are at once bizarre and deeply familiar. Through elegant prose alive with stunning imagery, Diaz has crafted a novel that will haunt you long after the final page.

The boy stared with wide-eyed wonder as the circus tents bloomed up from the misty dawn like giant mushrooms come to life. He clutched his guardian's hand tightly, scarcely believing he'd been allowed to attend the show. After so many whispered stories of sideshow freaks and death-defying acts, he would finally see the spectacle for himself.

As the sun burned off the morning fog, a kaleidoscope of sights, sounds and smells dazzled the boy's senses. Roars rumbled from animal cages while vendors sang out about sugared treats. Bold circus posters depicted fire-eaters, sword-swallowers, a wolfman, a bearded woman, a turtle boy and more. What strange creatures awaited him inside the striped big top?

The boy remembered his schoolmates jeering at him, calling him a "freak." But here, could the freaks walk openly, without shame? The idea filled him with awe.

A gruff voice interrupted his musings - it was time for the show to start. The boy hurried inside, clutching his ticket stub like a golden ticket. The tent flaps swept closed behind him with a whisper, and the lights dimmed...

As foreboding organ notes crept through the heavy air, the ringmaster stalked into the spotlight, cracked his whip, and proclaimed, "Ladies and gentlemen, welcome to the greatest show on earth!"

Read more at https://twitter.com/Francisco_Ecofa.

Lazarus - rip
Kira and the Ice Storm

Watch for more at https://twitter.com/Francisco_Ecofa.

About the Author

Francisco Angulo Madrid, 1976

Enthusiast of fantasy cinema and literature and a lifelong fan of Isaac Asimov and Stephen King, Angulo starts his literary career by submitting short stories to different contests. At 17 he finishes his first book - a collection of poems – and tries to publish it. Far from feeling intimidated by the discouraging responses from publishers, he decides to push ahead and tries even harder.

In 2006 he published his first novel "The Relic", a science fiction tale that was received with very positive reviews. In 2008 he presented "Ecofa" an essay on biofuels, whereAngulorecounts his experiences in the research project he works on. In 2009 he published "Kira and the Ice Storm".A difficultbut very productive year, in2010 he completed "Eco-fuel-FA",a science book in English. He also worked on several literary projects: "The Best of 2009-2010", "The Legend of Tarazashi 2009-2010", "The Sniffer 2010", "Destination Havana 2010-2011" and "Company No.12".

He currently works as director of research at the Ecofa project. Angulo is the developer of the first 2nd generation biofuel obtained from organic waste fed bacteria. He specialises in environmental issues and science-fiction novels.

His expertise in the scientific field is reflected in the innovations and technological advances he talks about in his books, almost prophesying what lies ahead, as Jules Verne didin his time.

Francisco Angulo Madrid-1976

Gran aficionado al cine y a la literatura fantástica, seguidor de Asimov y de Stephen King, Comienza su andadura literaria presentando relatos cortos a diferentes certámenes. A los 17 años termina su primer libro, un poemario que intenta publicar sin éxito. Lejos de amedrentarse ante las respuestas desalentadoras de las editoriales, decide seguir adelante, trabajando con más ahínco.

Read more at https://twitter.com/Francisco_Ecofa.